The Tennis Players

Also by Lars Gustafsson

The Death of a Beekeeper
(Translated by Janet K. Swaffar
and Guntram H. Weber)

Lars Gustafsson

The Tennis Players

Translated from the Swedish
by Yvonne L. Sandstroem

A NEW DIRECTIONS BOOK

To my friends
John and Joel,
Bob and Larry,
Janet and Frankie

Originally published as *Tennisspelarna* by P. A. Nordstedt and Söners Förlag, Stockholm, in 1977. This English translation is published by arrangement with Carl Hanser Verlag, Munich.

Assistance for the translation of this volume was given by The Swedish Institute, Stockholm, whose support is gratefully acknowledged.

Manufactured in the United States of America
First published clothbound and as New Directions Paperbook 551 in 1983
Published simultaneously in Canada by George J. McLeod, Ltd., Toronto

Library of Congress Cataloging in Publication Data
Gustafsson, Lars, 1936–
    The tennis players.
    (A New Directions Book)
    Translation of: Tennisspelarna.
    I. Title.
PT9876.17.U8T413   1983   839.7'374   82-22559
ISBN 0-8112-0861-3
ISBN 0-8112-0862-1 (pbk.)

New Directions Books are published for James Laughlin
by New Directions Publishing Corporation,
80 Eighth Avenue, New York 10011

1. Siegfried's Rhine Journey

Yes. It was a happy time. Now, long afterward, I see clearly that it was a happy time.

I used to get up about six while there was still some coolness in the air, pull on my shirt and a pair of very faded jeans, and put a tennis racket, six balls, Nietzsche's *Beyond Good and Evil* and a volume of Brandes' *Major Movements in the Literature of the Nineteenth Century* into my backpack. Then I'd pick up my Italian bike, a ten-speed Italo Vega, a real beauty, from the parking garage in my apartment house where a gigantic padlock chained it to an enormous concrete pillar and rush out into the morning light, which was still rose colored.

As a rule I didn't return to my apartment until nine, just in time for the last news from CBS featuring the paternally concerned Walter Cronkite and all the junk about depression, unemployment, and devaluation. At night, when it was cool again, I'd write; I wrote a lot in Austin, in south central Texas.

Then, in October, it was often ninety or even ninety-five degrees in the afternoon, with razor-sharp shadows and an immense white sea of light floating above the entire area. It was as if reflections from the great desert country to the southwest had somehow reached the hills and trees of Travis County, transforming the sunlight into an even stronger, even more unnaturally glowing white heat.

But the mornings were quite different; they had a fine, almost brittle quality, and I have never seen anything like the sunrises in south central Texas.

1

Never, either before or after, have I been in such great physical shape as I was there. I remember that I always used to whistle "Siegfried's Rhine Journey" from *Götterdämmerung* while pedaling up even the steepest hills on my ten-speed.

There are very few pieces of music as ill-suited to whistling. Actually, the best parts of "Siegfried's Rhine Journey" are written for trombone and for a special kind of long tuba called a Wagner tuba.

I heard all this inside of me as I went along on my bike. But if anyone had been listening to me as I pedaled up the steep hills, still wet with dew—he'd have heard nothing but a faint peep.

There were other amusing differences. "Siegfried's Rhine Journey" deals with a Norse hero on his way down a dark, foggy river toward strange Germanic adventures in gathering gloom, while I journeyed, in light that steadily increased in strength and brightness, toward the tennis court in a part of town on the other side of Lamar Boulevard.

The court was very simple. Squeezed in behind a public school, with a horrendous fruit and vegetable stand called Fred's Vegetables on the other side, was a park, a very small, not particularly neat park. And in the middle of this park, shaded by pecan trees whose hard nuts fell in drifts all over the asphalt, causing certain problems, was this very simple tennis court. The concrete was uneven, and the net was chicken wire, which had become rather rusty and would tear your pants if they got caught on it in the course of a particularly intense duel at the net.

At this time of morning, around seven o'clock, the

2

court was usually deserted, and I would practice my serve there in peace and quiet for an hour before I went to deliver my morning lecture in a course entitled Friedrich Nietzsche and Nineteenth-Century Scandinavia.

Around eight a crowd of people would show up from different directions. I'm quite sure they didn't know a thing about each other; some arrived on bikes and others in large, rattling Chryslers with loose headlights and bumpers; they started playing doubles and singles indiscriminately on the two cement courts. Boys and girls, young people in jeans and T-shirts, with funny slogans printed on them, different players each time. I got the impression that there were some who spent all day under the pecan trees.

About this time, I'd have to bike to my lecture at the university, but I always had time to exchange a few simple, friendly words with them. I thought it was the nice thing to do. Some of the girls played remarkably good tennis, and there was an extremely tall black who apparently came there often. He had a small dark mustache. I only saw the beginning of the game, but I got the impression that he belonged in the Wimbledon Open or the Forest Hills singles finals rather than on a concrete court in a run-down suburban park.

But just as their game was getting properly under way I always had to throw myself on my bike in order to be at my lectern at the precise moment when the bells in the beautiful white tower right in the middle of the immense university grounds were playing *Freude, schöner Götterfunken, Tochter aus Elysium* from Beethoven's Ninth. Tanned and fit as a young god, with my racket in one hand and a pile of books in the other, I climbed my

3

lectern, making a springboard dive, a violent somersault, into another continent, another century, into a world where Nietzsche still walks with Lou Salomé, where summer comes across the Starnbergersee, where Strindberg's guitar twangs in the smoke of Zum Schwarzen Ferkel in a Berlin so filled with genius and coal smoke that the sky is as dark as the darkness in the black eyes of the Polish writer-in-exile Przybyszewski, a time of false dogma, disappointments, heterodoxy, and strange elitist theories: a time when intellectuals are getting tired of beating their foreheads bloody against the wall of lies and instead start asking themselves if perhaps lies and truths come to the same thing in the end.

A time of coal smoke and absinthe, when Europe starts to give up hope, when every moral obligation is being questioned by brave souls in sepia attics and during walks along the idyllic shores of Lago Maggiore, lined with health resorts.

A time when our own catastrophes are being prepared.

I'm quite convinced that there are other inhabited planets. Not other planets in our solar system, but a conveniently situated planet here and there among the other, innumerable other solar systems.

Simply for reasons of probability, one has to assume that some of those beings who inhabit other planets are our superiors.

My thesis that there must be intellectually and morally superior beings on other planets is based on ethics rather than on astrophysical fact. Allowing humanity to represent the highest intellectual and moral level would be an unpardonable blunder on the part of the undeniably

4

gifted eccentric who has created the universe. I suspect that Nietzsche meant nothing more than this, but just try to explain that to American students. In English, *Übermensch* has to be translated as "Superman," and Superman is nothing but a character in the comics whose adventures we have all followed in our childhood at some kitchen table or other, a Fascistoid policeman who changes into tights in telephone booths and takes part in all the big police actions. A member of the Police Reserve, in other words.

There are hundreds of Reserve Policemen in every American city. They carry a special kind of heavy, watertight flashlight that can be used as a nightstick. In the sixties, they always used to be called up every time there were racial disturbances: they were drawn from approximately the same group as the subscribers to those brightly colored gun magazines one sees on all the newsstands.

When you are lecturing to American students about Nietzsche, you've got to watch your step. Otherwise you might easily teach them that Nietzsche was a German with a large mustache who invented the Police Reserve.

August Strindberg and Georg Brandes are then reduced to a Swede and a Dane blindly adoring a German who invented the Police Reserve.

If you continue in that vein for any length of time, you'll find that the audience at your lectures has thinned out considerably.

Mine were a success. I don't know how many times we had to change to a larger lecture hall. The only time in my life I've felt that I enjoyed solid popularity and a large audience was during my tenure as Visiting Professor of

5

Scandinavian Literature in Austin, Texas. I never quite grasped the reason for this, but it's the truth. I liked it a lot. After that experience, I have never said or written anything derogatory about the U.S. In point of fact, I make only one demand on humanity, but that one's rather strict: they've got to love me.

If I protest against bloody colonial wars it's mostly because I feel that anyone who can do something like that would be capable of treating me the same way.

There was one other professor in Austin as popular as I was. He was an Indian guru who, during the course of a very long and complicated series of lectures, demonstrated that all of reality is an illusion created by ourselves. Consequently it is possible to change reality radically by using a slightly improved breathing technique. I never went to his lectures, so I don't know whether he considered breathing technique to be illusory as well. But it is true that on one occasion, when I inadvertently tried to put a seminar on Strindberg's *Inferno* in the same time slot as his, it almost caused a campus riot.

I notice that I have strayed too far from my topic, the intellectually and morally superior inhabitants of other planets.

What I wanted to say is, suppose some such superior being were to come here—he probably wouldn't find much to admire. Skyscrapers—bah! A thousand-plane raid against Dresden in February of 1945—damnable! Atom bombs—obscene. Henrik Abel's proof of the partial insolvability of fourth-class equations—sure, pal.

There are actually only two things that I can imagine such a visitor admiring. One is Mozart's *Don Giovanni*. The other is the tennis serve.

6

In world tournaments, the Australian Open for instance, it may happen that a player makes three double faults in a row.

This says something about the degree of difficulty. No one really knows how to serve. You know in theory, of course, but nobody who's just about to make a serve can feel confident of his success. There's really only one way, and that is to commit yourself to the dark, wordless side of your personality, to rely on it and leave it the hell alone. Only then will you be able to carry through the breath-taking act of muscular co-ordination, thousandth-of-an-inch adjustments of wrists, ankles, and back muscles which constitute a serve.

The tennis serve is a window to the unknown.

I'm not quite sure what happened, but in the fall of 1974, when I suddenly found myself a Visiting Professor at the University of Texas at Austin, in the shade of mighty elms and soft green pecans, surrounded by students with beards and jeans and flowing locks, with the rest of the world, the rest of my experiences pleasantly submerged beyond an endless horizon of dusty semidesert and ocean, that fall I got completely captivated by tennis.

It wasn't enough for me to play a couple of hours a day—toward the end I subscribed to two different tennis magazines, and every week I used at least five different courts. A respectable collection of rackets made from all kinds of materials and of different degrees of tension filled my closet. Above the bookshelves in my office at the university sweaty tennis shirts were always drying in the mild breeze from the Mexican Gulf.

My tan was as dark as a black man's, and I had to take

a close look at my body in the mornings in order to recognize it. I was able to run up six flights of stairs in the university library, carrying a heavy briefcase, whistling the "Fire Music" from the end of *Die Walküre* at the same time.

Only rarely did I speak to my colleagues about anything but tennis. Since none of them had known me the way I was in Europe, they all took it as a matter of course. Since they were convinced that I was someone who had never lived for anything but sports, they always took me to all the college games: football, basketball, raquetball, handball, and God knows what: they discussed the latest televised football games with me endlessly, and of course this led to my having to watch more and more football games on TV.

As the months progressed, a completely different personality crystallized in me, a total stranger, but not at all unpleasant; he was somewhat limited, perhaps, in his fanatical sports interest, but quite likable on the whole. Sometimes I miss him. I wonder where he went. Nowadays I play tennis about once every other week with some sportswriter on the *Vestmanlands Läns Tidning*, and as a rule, I lose. They display polite surprise that a thin, nonathletic bellyacher like me can play tennis at all.

They don't know what they're missing. In the beginning of 1974, in Santa Barbara, I played against a California tournament player who'd just returned from Forest Hills. It's true that I lost two sets out of three, but the one I did win, I won 6–1, and those I lost, I lost 7–5, 7–5.

Shortly after that I returned to my usual medocrity, in large part because I started to get really scared by the whole thing. However, the fact remains: late in 1974, I was able to keep a California tournament player, the kind who enters the court with six rackets under his arm, at bay for a whole set.

I remember his serve quite well. It flashed in the sunlight; the sound of his steel racket with specially tightened natural stringing echoed off the sunny walls of the University of Santa Barbara. The ball came at me like a yellow streak where I crouched about four yards behind the base line, quiet, forgetting all the world. A serve like that gives the receiver about 0.3 seconds to make up his mind what to do.

I remember how I used to stand and watch it coming at me, how the whole world was transformed into a single object, a tennis ball. As yet it was slightly egg-shaped, deformed by the stroke. The seams of the ball made strange patterns during the rapid right-hand spins. After clearing the net, the ball had time to rotate eight times.

After the bounce it hung suspended in the air, a wordless challenge in a world beyond words. It seemed to be saying, "In reality you are no one."

Until a long hard backhand along the left-hand line carried this unbearable and liberating truth away from me once more.

Of course it wasn't enough for me to play tennis, read tennis magazines, talk tennis. I also dreamed all night of long, complicated games against an invisible but apparently devilishly clever opponent.

Every morning after a game like that I'd wake up with a severe case of tennis elbow.

2. A Couple of Clouds in My Sky

The stupefying afternoon heat pressed down on the lawn under the tall bell tower. I was sitting in the shade of a large pecan tree next to the dean's house, listening to exotic birds chattering with strange metallic voices in the trees above me. The only people in view were two students, both black, playing Frisbee back and forth across the lawn.

I don't know whether you know about Frisbee. It's the game of the future. When all our old European ball-games have died out, Frisbee will dominate the world. It was invented before the First World War at a coffee factory in the Midwest called Frisbee's. That brand of coffee came in round cans, and the cans had lids with turned-down rims. Those lids were piled in a yard where the workmen would sit after lunch. By and by, they started to play around with them. They soon discovered that the turned-down rim invested the lid with fabulous aerodynamic qualities. It rises, falls, swings in gentle parabolas according to initial speed, angle, positive or negative spin at launching, and six or seven other variables that I'm not familiar with.

The behavior of those lids is almost as remarkable as that of elementary particles. Now there are Frisbees of all kinds, and the most expensive cost about twenty-five dollars. For the generation after the drug generation, they seem capable of consuming whole afternoons. Obviously, it's not a competitive game: on the contrary, the point is to launch your Frisbee on a long, complicated flight, but not so complicated that your partner can't receive it. If it falls to the ground it's a failure not just for one player, but for both.

With a sigh, I closed August Strindberg's *Inferno.* I had read it all the way through; it had taken a long hot Texas afternoon, and the whole time, that little red disc had buzzed across the emerald grass between the two black muscular bodies that should have been securely anchored to a couple of desks in the library.

A cowboy in a wide-brimmed hat and sparkling boots stomped across the gravel in front of my bench, where a couple of strange-looking yellow-tailed sparrows had been hopping about.

The cowboy moved with determined gait. When the clock high up in the bell tower struck five, he looked at his own silver turnip pocketwatch and put on speed. Naturally the gleaming black-leather holster on his belt didn't contain a Colt or a Peacemaker but an SR-51 from Texas Instruments. It had taken quite a long time for me to grasp that all those people on campus who carried heavy black-leather holsters on their belts kept minicomputers in them. Fabulous little gadgets that can calculate arcs, hyperbolic tangents, logarithms, permutations, the square root of five, and the immediate compound interest of whatever number you like before you even have a chance to turn around.

Those cowboys were all young scientists from the College of Engineering, and they were all what you might call trigger-happy. Right in the middle of a conversation, one of them would suddenly pull out his SR-51 and throw himself into prodigious computations.

As I've already mentioned, the clock in the bell tower struck five and—as happened twice a day—the delicate

11

bells at the top of the yellow sandstone building, narrow and two hundred feet high, played the "Ode to Joy" from Beethoven's Ninth.

> *Freude, schöner Götterfunken,*
> *Tochter aus Elysium,*
> *Wir betreten feuertrunken,*
> *Himmlische, dein Heiligtum.*

It's an impressive building. First there are four floors occupied by the university administration. There President Alfred Sperr and his lawyers and advisers and friends and great-looking blonde secretaries sit administering a budget of one billion dollars.

The next fifteen floors hide the accumulations of Western culture in the shape of a gigantic university library. There are millions of books, very closely packed on shelves that go right up to the ceiling in dim rooms lit by plain light fixtures, protected by wire cages, all the way up to the eighteenth floor. Moving around in the bookish dimness inside this tower was a fascinating experience. Going up in the tiny, very slow, and cramped elevator that rattled its way up through the masses of books felt like going up through a tube of toothpaste. I often had a feeling of horror as I moved from floor to floor, hunting for some forgotten nineteenth-century philosopher or for my favorite student, Doobie Smith from Dallas. She would sit at a small, badly lit table, covered by yard-high piles of books, exhibiting a strange resemblance to the few preserved portraits of Lou Salomé, the lady whom Nietzsche loved and who gave rise to the expression *die Blonde Bestie*. Around this time in the afternoon I used to pick her up for a cup of coffee in the extraordinary shopping center close to campus which, strangely enough, was called Doobie Mall.

I could imagine her up there, cut off from the Orphic light whose brilliance bathed the outside of the tower, with her wise little blonde head resting on her chubby hand and her steel-blue eyes myopically stumbling across the pages of Hartmann's *Philosophy of the Unconscious.*

The tower had a strange fascination for the students. My own terror was closely related to claustrophobia, to a feeling that any time now a terrible mine disaster would occur in this narrow shaft of centuries, that Europe's and America's collected literary sediment would crumble, fall through floor after floor and bury me underneath like an ant who has ended up under a mound of sand some truck has unloaded.

The students' fascination, however, was of a different kind. It belonged to the category of things which made them somehow strange to me.

Every time the football team, the Texas Longhorns, won a game, the top of the tower would be lit by strong red lights, which definitely made it look like a stiff, erect, male member, an ecstatic phallus which was even visible from the air as you came in for a landing.

At that time eight students had jumped from the tower. This was something which had started in 1966, more precisely on a beautiful 100-degree June day. It was lunchtime; people were streaming out of the university buildings and across the lawn; lots of people were on their way under the trees, going in different directions to their usual lunch stops. It was, as I have already said, an unusually hot June day, and the clock in the tower struck twelve.

13

Among those walking across the lawn, whose center was marked by a huge flagpole from which the Texas flag drooped for lack of wind, was a prominent English nuclear physicist who was visiting one of the labs.

Suddenly something unexpected happened. The Englishman faltered, took another step, an uncertain gliding step as if he'd slipped on a banana peel, and fell down. Since a banana peel on this lawn was as unthinkable as an elk at a Nobel banquet, those closest to him came to the conclusion that something serious had happened. Some people politely went to help him up. They discovered that where the back of the man's head should have been there was nothing but a large, gaping hole. They looked up and around.

Everything looked quite normal. The lawn was full of students dressed in jeans and loose shirts, lazily stretched out on the grass, eating sandwiches, talking, petting, engrossed in their books. Beards, long dark hair, handsome well-exercised bodies.

A Renoir might have done justice to this picture: these creatures spread out on the emerald grass, at once vulnerable and strong, strangely helpless and at the same time full of a fascinating optimism whose source I have never quite fathomed.

I know exactly what it might have looked like on that June day. I often think sadly of how many beautiful young people like them had to be buried in foreign Asiatic soil because of an insane, criminal war.

Some things about them never cease to amaze me. Their emotional brittleness, their perfect tennis serves, their almost frightening capability of grasping things: Gunnar Ekelöf's Akrit poems, non-Abelian groups, and Nietzsche's *Beyond Good and Evil*, almost in the same breath; their strange conviction that the world outside of Texas is meant for war and tourism.

That's the way it may have looked that afternoon. Everyone went on talking happily as before. A medical student leaned competently over the huge wound in the back of the dead Englishman's head in order to get a better look at the gray matter of the brain.

He shouldn't have done that. Soon he, too, rested.

Inside of thirty minutes thirteen of those people would be dead. None of them knew it until the moment his turn had come.

Actually, thirteen isn't quite correct, since two were ambulance men who tried to carry away the wounded.

An ex-marine, a Boy Scout leader and gun enthusiast— he had been going to the university psychiatrist for a couple of months and was regarded as someone who was clearly getting better—and who can prove that he wasn't? —he had spent the afternoon killing his mother and had then barricaded himself in the tower. He had put four high-powered rifles with telescopic sights on the ledge, one for each point of the compass, probably acting on the belief that to someone who has killed his mother, the whole world is open.

The gunfight that erupted when the National Guard and every policeman in Travis County were in position was quite lively. Toward the end they directed at the tower burst after burst from heavy machine guns mounted on armored cars. You could hear the metallic clang of bullets ricocheting against the marble cornice. An old professor lay low for two hours behind the roots of the huge tree which, on this peaceful afternoon, shaded my seat. In the doorway over there a student got a cramp in his leg. He was lying almost directly in the line of fire when

15

the shooting started and threw himself into a doorway, only to discover that some idiot had panicked, locked the door from the inside, and shot the bolt. And he didn't dare pull his leg into the narrow space between the doorposts for fear that his movement would be noticeable in the gun's telescopic sights.

Heavily armored helicopters made repeated passes at the top of the tower but had no success.

Those hours of paralysis, horror, and madness ended as suddenly as they had begun. A young deputy sheriff simply took the elevator up through all the library floors; he passed through all eighteen floors of collected culture in the creaking elevator and calmly stepped out onto the viewing platform on the nineteenth floor. When he opened the elevator doors, the killer was standing on the other side of the balcony, completely engrossed in his telescopic sights.

The sheriff killed him with a single, well-aimed shot. Actually, the dead man's dossier didn't contain anything out of the ordinary. His was a rather ordinary case of study-neurosis.

But now the afternoon was peaceful; the students had gone home; the clock in the tower had struck five, and I had an hour before the start of my seminar. I would just have time for a cup of coffee. And I'd just started to dream about having one of those really fat, apple-filled donuts that usually lay on a stoneware plate in the window of the coffee shop, when Doobie turned up. She carried some heavy tomes under her right arm; her wise blue eyes were narrowed against the afternoon light, and the sun poured light into her reddish-blonde hair. She really looked amazingly like Lou Salomé.

16

Born in Dallas, and actually a product of the Baptist college in San Antonio, this girl, who had never set foot in Europe, sometimes showed such a profound understanding of the history of ideas in nineteenth-century Europe that I occasionally wondered whether the ridiculous theory of reincarnation might not be true after all. Brandes, Nietzsche, Weininger, Max Stirner, August Strindberg—she spoke of them all like old friends and perceived their arguments as something happening here and now. She had become a competent reader of Norwegian so that she would be able to understand Ibsen; she read Danish in order to understand J. P. Jacobsen, and her German was full of strangely antiquated slang from the Berlin of the 1870s.

I always suspected that one of the strongest reasons for her interest in me was that I was a Scandinavian author who had spent a couple of years in voluntary exile in Berlin. When we talked about that city, we got into some strange arguments. For her, Berlin was still a city of gaslights and dark hansom cabs going through cobbled streets. She would get impatient with me because I didn't know literary coffee shops that now exist only as building materials for some hundred feet of the Wall. Things like that were a bit difficult to explain to her.

The intriguing thing about her was that she was a kid from Dallas, and at the same time she wasn't. She knew more about Europe than I do, but her Europe and mine were strangely dissimilar.

What else can I tell you about Doobie? Lots of things, but I'm not going to tell you all of them. She was a Nietzschean, one of the most committed Nietzscheans I've ever met, not in any vulgar, conservative sense, but seriously. She really believed that truth is that which

17

serves life and that as far as morals are concerned, we have to invent our own if we find ourselves in a situation where it suddenly occurs to us that we are in need of morals.

I won't deny that this friendship was good for me.

Every morning, after my early tennis practice, showered and with a large dose of coffee in my stomach, I'd descend to the lobby of the somewhat peculiar apartment complex where I lived, try to avoid the extremely talkative old ladies who slumped in the lobby chairs from sunup to sundown talking about their grandchildren in Colorado and in Milwaukee, and check my mailbox. Papers and mail from Sweden, crashing down at irregular intervals, were always lively reminders of what happens when it's the other way around, when your morals are much too rigid for the situation in which you find yourself.

The building superintendent, who distributed the mail, was an old bantamweight from New Orleans; he himself always maintained that his father had been born a slave. At any rate, I'd usually get the Swedish mail out of my system by shadowboxing with him for a couple of rounds. As a boxer, he was incredibly fast and competent, almost impossible to hit, and when he'd accidentally connect, I could feel it all the way to the roots of my teeth. He was a strangely happy man who would be on the move in that enormous building from seven in the morning until nine at night, always dragging along a huge toolbox with pliers, soldering irons, and lead hammers. The only bad thing about him was his habit of whistling Beethoven's *Für Elise*. It is not suitable for whistling.

He was one of only two blacks that I knew in Austin. The other one was a graduate student in my seminar, very black, very tall, very skinny, and quite mad. He was the reason I had spent a long hot Texas afternoon reading August Strindberg's *Inferno*—how many times I had read

18

it God only knows. For Bill was a Strindberg man and he'd had an idea, so brilliant and so damn bizarre that should he be able to prove it, Strindberg criticism would be rocked to its foundations forever after.

This is how it was:

In 1898, Strindberg's novel *Inferno* was published in Paris. As everyone knows, it deals with how the author flees from his Austrian wife, Frida Uhl, how he settles down in a shabby room in the Hotel Orfila in Paris and throws himself into a series of alchemical experiments which he had been preparing for a long time. He wants to prove that sulfur is no simple elementary matter but a kind of coal compound. After a few days and nights in front of the roaring tile stove his hands are scaly and bloody from the heat; he lands in the hospital for a while; a French chemist affirms the correctness of his analysis. Now things start happening at the Hotel Orfila as dear August gets more and more engrossed in his great, definitive work, namely making gold. Mysterious characters move into the apartment above his; every time he moves his chair he can hear some object being moved in the apartment above. Strange boxes that seem to contain electrical equipment are dragged up the stairs, more and more electrical equipment every day. Poor August starts to suffer from anxiety: he feels a weight on his chest and can't sleep until he has changed rooms. His apprehensive feelings about electrically staged attacks become stronger, and—well, that's the start of what is referred to as Strindberg's Inferno Crisis.

Some literary historians have explained it as an outbreak of paranoia which only subsides years later, when Strindberg is able to anchor his world in the Christian dogma of sin. Others have seen *Inferno* as, above all, a very imaginative and amusing symbolic novel, strongly influenced by various vulgar ideas that were floating around in the dim light of magic and superstition that pervades French literature around the turn of the century.

All this is, I almost said just as it should be, and the result is one of the maddest and most fascinating novels in Swedish literature, the kind of novel that makes it possible to support yourself as a Visiting Professor at foreign universities when the atmosphere at home becomes too stifling. August's *Inferno* is okay. The scholars' theories are okay.

And then this damn Bill, blacker and thinner and more excited than ever, bursts into my study two days before and puts a small dusty volume with damp-spotted covers on my desk. Very cheap covers, sleazy gray paper.

"Read this," he says.

"Why?"

"Man, it's sensational. It'll interest you."

"Fuck you, I don't have time to read all the damn books students drag in. What kind of junk is this?" (I let my fingers slide across the front cover; the paper was unusually rough and disagreeable to the touch.)

The author's name on the title page was almost illegible because of the damp spots, but I made it out to be something like Pietziewzskoczsky. I wondered how it should be pronounced.

Zygmunt I. Pietziewzskoczsky
MEMOIRES D'UN CHIMISTE

"Let me have a look at it," I said. "Perhaps I'll find time to read it. Paris 1899—h'm, is there anything there that might be of interest to Strindberg scholars?"

I pushed it into my backpack between my tennis rackets and indicated to Bill that the audience was over. He looked even slyer than usual as he left.

I started reading the book on my couch in front of the TV that same night. Casually, I turned off Walter Cronkite and poured myself a bourbon. I finished reading, bone tired, at dawn the following day, fell asleep with a head like lead, and didn't wake up until lunchtime. When I did wake up I took for granted that I'd been dreaming; unfortunately, such was not the case.

There was no doubt. Pietziewzskoczsky, let's call him Zygmunt from here on for the sake of simplicity, well Zygmunt was a Polish chemist in exile, born in Cracow in 1823. I'll skip his biography: his childhood in Cracow, the rather amusing tales from his time at a Polish university, his war experiences, his contacts with cells of anarchists in Poland and Russia, his memories of 1848, his long, intense friendship with Stanslaw Przybyszewski, Strindberg's friend from Zum Schwarzen Ferkel in Berlin, the one who gradually turned into a rival and, eventually, a mortal enemy.

To get to the point: in one of its last chapters, this strange memoir contains a complete confession of how it all happened. August was on the right track to begin with: both he and his readers turned out to be mistaken. There was a group of anarchists, Poles in exile, friends of Przybyszewski's, who gathered in the apartment above Strindberg's in the Hotel Orfila. Their aim was not to kill him but to find the secret behind his alchemy. They wanted to overturn the social order by throwing huge amounts of gold francs on the French market. That August was almost killed was simply due to their experiments with some kind of gas which, introduced into his

21

apartment from the one above through a ventilator, was intended to put him into a sleep just deep enough so that they could make off with his notes.

They had carried on this questionable activity almost throughout the Inferno Crisis. Zygmunt ascribes the fact that they had eluded detection to nothing more than August's naïve conviction that he was the center of the universe, and so he naturally had to assume the *Powers* were persecuting him.

On the inside back cover was the library stamp. Of course the book originated on one of the upper floors of the university library. Its classification was CHEMISTRY: PRE-TWENTIETH CENTURY.

Not so strange, after all, that nobody had found it before.

"Well, well," I said to myself. "That's that."

And now there was only one hour before the start of the seminar where Bill, black, alert, and scornful, would want to hear my opinion. My prestige was seriously endangered.

"Let's go," I said to Doobie, who tucked herself cozily under my right arm, "let's go get some coffee. I've got a problem."

"So do I," she said.

3. Backhand Down the Line

Exactly twenty-two minutes past seven in the morning, two days later, I put my key into the padlock in the garage and liberated my ten-speed Italo Vega from the mighty chain that fettered it to the wall. It was cool enough so that I still had to wear a wool sweater, and I had goose pimples on my bare legs. Not too bad, though, for a December morning, I thought, while the derailleur moved the chain from one sprocket to another, soft as a whisper, while I went down the floor of the garage at steadily gathering speed.

Two blue-haired ladies in a huge Cadillac waved at me encouragingly on the ground floor as I passed a fraction of an inch in front of their bumper.

I slid into the traffic on Nineteenth Street, which was already heavy, among gigantic trailer trucks from which long-horned cattle peered curiously through the slats and mooed in tones intended for endless prairies and wide horizons.

While the chain kept jumping onto larger and larger sprockets, I made it to the top of the hill and flew along the elegant bicycle path on San Jacinto Boulevard (for the last ten years, every new candidate for city office in Austin has had more bicycle paths on his program), turned into the small park behind the vegetable stand, and leaned my bike against the chicken-wire net on the tennis court.

There they were, and with a leap of joy I saw that there were only three of them; they seemed to have just arrived. They appeared to be in the process of warming up; long, deep shots went back and forth across the net with workmanlike precision. On one side stood a tall lanky guy with such thick glasses that I concluded he must be terribly nearsighted. He was dressed in a rather dirty shirt inscribed STRATEGIC AIR FORCE HANDBALL TEAM and a pair of cut-off jeans. He took turns with a small girl whose shirt said simply POLLY. She was one of the frailest, thinnest girls I've ever seen; her frailty made her seem almost unreal. It was a mystery how she could even handle a tennis racket. Her long brown hair was tied back in a little-girl red ribbon; around her incredibly thin wrists she wore heavy masculine sweatbands.

The hard, precise balls that the player on the other side of the net addressed alternately to the boy and to the girl whose name was Polly always landed exactly two inches from the base line. Polly sent them back, using a forehand every time, since she was standing in the deuce court, and it struck me that she had to be extremely good. The whole time she alternated topspin with slice; occasionally, when the ball hit a quarter of an inch closer to the base line, she hit a half-volley, so fast and precise that it was impossible to distinguish the sound of the ball bouncing against the raw concrete from the drier sound of the racket connecting.

The man on the other side of the net wore a leather hat. He was very tanned, his hair seemed blond, bleached by the sun, his face shaded by his hatbrim.

This player had one peculiarity. He never ran. He walked around the court with calm, springy steps, and whenever the ball landed he seemed to have lots of time to spare, even though he never seemed to increase the tempo of his footwork above ordinary walking speed.

He simply had to have a phenomenal capacity for anticipation. The players of the twenties and thirties had that capacity. Modern players seldom do. Instead they've developed their ability to hit on the move, without slowing down.

The ball must have come across the net thirty times before the lanky guy got a sudden freeze on one of his backhands and placed it in the net.

"Hello there," I said.

"Why don't you join us," said the lanky guy, nodding toward the man in the leather hat.

I pulled my tightly strung racket from my backpack. I noticed that it had massacred a copy of *Beyond Good and Evil* rather badly. Evidently it had served as a bookmark for the entire ride. It annoyed me. Absent-mindedly, I took the book with me onto the court.

"My name's Polly," said the girl.

"My name's Chris," said the lanky guy.

"My name's Abel," said the one with the leather hat. Now that I was close to the net I could see that his eyes were very red, as if he'd been staring into the sun too long, looking for fast balls.

"My name's Lars," I said. "Where do you want me to play?"

"Play with me," said Abel.

"I don't know, I'm not very good . . ."

"Man," said Abel, "don't talk. Let's play, and we'll see what happens."

I nodded and hit a couple of balls. My slice was fine, my backhand as hard and solid as it usually is (I always do difficult things better than easy ones, a habit my subconscious acquired in my youth; for example, I love to count non-Abelian groups and tensors but have never been able to divide a restaurant check). I always start with the most difficult and then laboriously climb down to easier stages, and if I can't do it that way I don't feel like doing it at all—I put my whole weight behind it, the steel

25

racket swung in that special, pleasing way, but every ball was returned, actually *every single ball.*

Polly always used two hands for her backhand; it looked a bit awkward, but when the ball came, it had power. Now and then Abel would walk out slowly to return a ball I'd missed. As soon as I tried to put a topspin on my balls they went into the net. It was the damnedest thing.

I lobbed a couple of good balls to see if they had any smash on the other side. It sounded like mortar fire exploding when the ball hit the metal net behind me after the bounce. I lobbed three of them, and every time the explosion followed.

I realized that those guys wouldn't be an easy match.

"Do you want to serve first," said Abel, who had watched every move I'd made with a kind of neutral interest.

"O.K.," I said, "let me have a couple of balls."

At that time I had an American Twist that wasn't too bad. I'd use it for my second serve when nothing else helped. It would land far to the right and kind of creep along the base line.

I decided to try that. Evidently Chris would be the receiver.

I hate to start serving against unknown opponents, and these were clearly three or four degrees out of my league. The queen in chess is like the serve in tennis. No other move has such a large degree of license; nothing is as catastrophic as a bad serve, and nothing is as successful as an effective one.

Furthermore, there's nothing as revealing as a serve. It tells the degree of your self-confidence, your power, your control of the ball, your concentration—everything.

There's nothing more public than a tennis serve. Compared to a tennis serve, a confessional novel in a woman's magazine is like a combination safe.

Unfortunately, that's the way it is. *Don't blame me*, as Strindberg's Dr. Borg says, *I didn't make those laws.*

"O.K.," I said, and held up the ball for the guy called Chris.

It was a nice toss, precisely in line with my left ear, just as far to the left as the toss for an American Twist ought to lie to get the correct, perverse lateral spin.

The ball hung there. It was quite worn, a yellow High Pressure Dunlop. It rotated in a slow left-hand spin against the Texas winter sky. Somewhere behind my left ear the head of my racket was already moving into the second half of the strange oar stroke which is a tennis serve, and consequently my whole weight was shifting to my left foot and rolling the way ocean waves roll toward the shore.

Empty, happily empty, like a zero, like a sign without meaning, the ball just hung there, and something inside of me congratulated me on its emptiness. Somewhere in the emptiness a bird twittered in the branches of the large pecan tree overhanging the court.

For a Dallas girl, Doobie was amazingly hard up. She lived with her sister, and since her sister was one of the most brilliant harpists in all of southern Texas, with lots of pupils and concert engagements, Doobie usually did all right too.

But now it was the fall of 1974. Every single day, dozens of car dealers and building contractors in Travis County went out of business, and the menswear stores along Guadalupe Street advertised super sales all the time, and for some reason the business slowdown also seemed to affect harp solos. Something like that isn't easy to explain. It's hard to imagine a more solid little market than harp playing: small but solid. Either you like harp music or you don't. And if you like it you should be prepared to sacrifice for it. Beauty is the only thing that lasts, as all sensible people have realized for some time.

"You can say anything you want," said Doobie, "but the simple truth is that Elizabeth can't afford me any longer. She doesn't have a cent either."

She dipped her third apple donut into her coffee and sucked it lustily. I looked at her, moved. She was the only Nietzschean I had ever known, and there were times when I wished she had been my sister.

"Private lessons," I said.

"In what?"

"Scandinavian languages, the philosphy of the nine-teenth century, German, Ibsen, Brandes, Strindberg, Jacobsen—anything."

"Don't make jokes—people can't afford to go to Europe anymore, they can't even afford to go to Yucatan."

"Let me think," I said. "Sometimes I get good ideas. In my experience, as long as you don't think about money everything's all right. Then it all comes pouring in, but the trick is to watch it out of the corner of your eye; if you start staring, it gets frightened, like a shy girl."

"Don't sneer at my misfortune," said Doobie. "If nothing turns up, Elizabeth and I won't have the rent next month."

"Damn it, I've got to go to my seminar," I said. "Do you want to come?"

"It's about that damned French chemist who turned out to be the gang that persecuted Strindberg, right?"

"Yes," I said, "a very annoying affair. I'm not quite sure how to handle it. I haven't really got the kind of experience I need for this. By the way, isn't it strange that Bill, of all people, should find him? Damned bad luck, isn't it. You can't just ignore it. He'd just say it's *because he's black.* And just imagine the uproar when all the biographies have to be rewritten. And all because Bill couldn't stick to the course material."

"One thing strikes me," said Doobie. "That awful Pole, what's-his-name, the alchemy guy?"

"Zygmunt I. Pietziewzskoczsky."

"That's the one. Is it likely that Bill should be the first person to have discovered him? Couldn't there be one or two Strindberg scholars who've come across him before —isn't that quite probable, after all?

"What do you mean?"

"Like this: does the Paris Commune exist? That depends what you mean. There are a lot of events in and around Paris in 1870–71. They've been described as the *Paris Commune* for so long that any scholar who tried to question that concept would simply make a fool of himself. The same with Strindberg's Inferno Crisis. It's been a historical fact for a long time."

"What are you getting at?"

(Her intelligence, which was extreme, didn't always make it easy for the rest of us to follow her. She was always a step ahead; it wouldn't have been so annoying if it hadn't been that every time you took the step, Doobie had taken *another one.*)

"What I mean is that it would still have been possible

to do away with Strindberg's Inferno Crisis in the twenties, but anyone who tries it now, he'd simply make a *fool* of himself. There are just too many people who have built their careers on the Inferno Crisis, who make their living teaching about it. You can't drag in some old Polish alchemist at this point, that would be as ridiculous as trying to prove that the Russian Revolution ended early in 1918. Believe me, sensible people have seen that memoir long ago and decided to disregard it."

"Do you really think so," I said, with an involuntary sigh of relief.

"Don't forget," Doobie added, here eyes glowing softly over the donuts, "don't forget that *only that which serves life is true*."

The seminar started just about the way I had imagined. It was unusually crowded, a lot of black friends of Bill's whom I hadn't seen before were there; they preferred to sit in the windows, which made the room dark. Quite a few of my colleagues had turned up as well. Professor John Weinstock, whose custom it was to take a nap every afternoon, twirled his moustache a few times. Then his heavy, musical snores, not unlike the beginning of a Bach cello suite, were diffused through the room. With a slight thud I allowed my books to land at the top of the table, shouted to the youngest teaching assistant to clean the blackboard, and started easily.

"1879: *The Red Room*. 1898: *Inferno*. What a hell of a lot of life, of experience there can be between two books in the life of the same author. And—don't forget this either—political and social changes. There are only seven years between the Paris Commune and *The Red Room*. A young man ventures forth, disguised as a journalist, to take a look at the society that he lives in. He sees that it is a society in which there is a striking discrepancy between public morals and the morals which in fact govern people's actions. He opens different doors, he looks into different rooms, and he observes that the same people seem to turn up in the different rooms. In other words, there seems to be a *conspiracy* behind society, a mysterious group of people, united by strong but invisible bonds. Everything that happens in society has two meanings, one open and visible, and another, which is hidden.

"1898: The Powers are no longer powers of society but metaphysical powers. Through his crisis, Strindberg arrives at the realization that the events in his life have two meanings, one openly visible and another, which is hidden. You might say, in other words," I said, carefully packing my pipe and lighting it—the students were always very interested in seeing whether I'd burn my fingers, and I'd always find something else to say before I brought the match to the bowl of my pipe—"that he accepts the thought that his life is governed by a conspiracy, but only after he has succeeded in transforming it into a metaphysical conspiracy. This is the meaning behind the concept of the *Powers* in Strindberg, those obscure but purposeful forces that . . ."

"That's a crock of shit!"

"What was that?"

(Already at an early stage I had discovered the necessity of taking my glasses off when such incidents occurred, polishing them carefully and peering in a trusting, disoriented manner at the corner from which the rebel was speaking. This almost always made him feel that he was, in some subtle way, *behaving badly*.)

"Oh, it's you, Bill. Please, you have the floor."

I have to admit that his organization wasn't bad. Occasionally one could see that I'd managed to teach him a thing or two. He did a run-through of Strindberg criticism from Böök to Smedmark, of course pronouncing the names of the Scandinavian scholars in horrible fashion, but he'd read them. He even managed to get in a few swipes at the Swedish Academy, at Governor Briscoe, and at President Sperr along the way, touched on the Watergate affair, and then let his find explode: *Mémoires d'un chimiste.* There really had been a gang in the Hotel Orfila that really had tried to do away with August Strindberg in hopes of getting their hands on his chemical secrets. Some international coal-and-gas syndicates that were being formed at this period carried on energetic research; the trade magazines, from the most academic to the alchemical ones, weird magazines like *L'Hyperchimie*, were subjected to the most painstaking examination by people hunting for new patents, and Strindberg's sulfur analysis, which proved that sulfur was not a chemical element but contained, among other things, large quantities of coal, evidently had inspired a French-Belgian mine consortium to hire some drunken Polish chemist to examine the whole thing.

Since they themselves, in spite of the most careful experiments, hadn't been able to find coal at the bottom of their crucibles, they had made up their minds to scratch in the bottom of Strindberg's instead. They had their contacts.

A few of them had actually been members of the Zum Schwarzen Ferkel group in Berlin some ten years earlier, that is to say, at the time when Strindberg and Przybyszewski were both in Berlin.

32

Przybyszewski himself studied chemistry extensively during his time in Berlin.

Didn't he himself say in his memoirs that for a long time he supported himself by writing dissertations for a firm that then sold them for a big price to graduate students who weren't up to writing their own doctoral theses? Anyway, one of them deals with chloroform and its effect on the central nervous system.

"And you know, we had a firm like that, specializing in the writing and selling of dissertations, right here in Austin, until second semester last year," he cleverly slipped in.

In brief, August Strindberg was on the right track for a short time at the beginning of his Inferno Crisis. A band of boozy Polish chemists-in-exile had occupied the room above his and tried to chloroform the Swedish writer in order to get their hands on his sulfur method.

As we've just heard, Przybyszewski himself was an expert on the effects of chloroform on the human body.

A real miracle, no, not a miracle but August's fanatical vigilance, his persecution complex, which made him look for just this kind of enemy activity, made the whole conspiracy come to nothing. Actually, a careful comparison of the two texts, *Inferno* and the Polish diary, would show how the battle had surged back and forth day by day—in brief, new light was undoubtedly being shed on the question of Strindberg's Inferno Crisis.

Of course there are still certain questions that might be asked. Many interesting questions. For example, why had the Polish gang suddenly given up and left the Hotel Orfila?

There were hints in the memoirs of the mysterious

Pietziewzskoczsky. He too had undergone a religious crisis, at first captivated by the occult movements current in the 1890s and then swiftly embracing Roman Catholicism, to end up finally as a monk in the Dominican monastery in Varna. Wasn't it repentance of that kind which seized him in the Hotel Orfila just as he was going to bore a hole through the ceiling of August's hotel room?

"Then what you're trying to say," I stated with ice-cold deliberation, sensuously filling my pipe, "is that we no longer have one Inferno Crisis to contend with but two: *Strindberg's and Pietziewzskoczsky's*."

Which was, if I may say so, rather a good dropball, and it took the wind out of him temporarily.

The room was very quiet. The blue smoke from my pipe swirled like intergalactic clouds just below the large round light fixtures. Two huge, angrily buzzing flies flew out of the largest cloud, close to one another.

I got the impression that they were doing something relatively indecent.

We were approaching the moment when someone absolutely had to say something.

It came from an unexpected quarter, from a small flabby guy with blue-black bristles and gold-rimmed glasses seated at the far end of the table. I'd never found out his name; perhaps it was Heinz or something along that line: he was from the East Coast originally, from Brooklyn. From the first day I'd felt a vague antipathy for him.

He was a bit too—European—for my taste. For instance, you'd never run across him in the gym, and he didn't even seem to follow college football.

Now he lifted up his voice and said, "You mentioned

34

something, Bill, that's so interesting that I wonder whether you even realize it yourself."

(Heinz always assumed that if someone happened to say something intelligent, it was by mistake.)

You could already hear Bill inhaling, then exhaling, in a snort. The flies were buzzing inside the smoke with increasing enthusiasm.

"So," said Bill.

"Well," said Heinz in a very aggressive tone of voice. "It was when you said that for long stretches it is possible to follow *Inferno* and *Memoirs of a Chemist* day by day. It opens up some interesting perspectives, I think."

(And he threw me a beseeching glance. I was completely absorbed in scratching out my pipe with my biggest and heaviest pocketknife. The spring before, I had used it in Västmanland for scraping paint off my boat, and it wasn't as sharp as it had been.)

"What do you have in mind," I asked.

"Running it through the computer, of course."

"What do you mean, *computer*? What good would that do?"

"You feed both books into a computer and program it to check the day-by-day correlation between the two narratives. If there is a real correlation between them, the computer will be able to map it out."

"Fun idea," I said. "But does this institution have access to computer time? I'll certainly have to look into that side of it."

At that moment, I was saved by the bell. We'd already gone over by half an hour.

I had a respite of eight days ahead of me. I had a strong feeling that I was going to need it.

35

4. Advantage Out

The ball! I knew there was something I had forgotten. Bright yellow, a gas-filled Dunlop, almost new, fuzzy and friendly, slowly rotating, almost sensuously exposing that funny pattern of seams that tennis balls have. As some of you may remember, it was the toss for my first serve in the first game of the first set of my first match with those characters who played tennis every morning in the little park next to Fred's Vegetables.

And there it's been hanging, steadfastly waiting, against a brilliant, thin-blue, Texas winter sky, for a whole chapter.

And down in the opposite corner, narrowing his eyes against the sun, was the guy I've called Chris, slowly rocking back and forth, prepared to receive my serve. He was tall and lanky, with incredibly long, calflike legs in bleached and torn tennis shorts. He wore the kind of almost spherical, very strong glasses that you only see on extremely nearsighted people. STRATEGIC AIR COMMAND HANDBALL TEAM!

And if I'd looked diagonally to my right I'd have seen Polly by the net, frail as a mosquito with her dancing braids, small and graceful in her cut-off jeans—how much sooner I'd have looked at her!

But now there was that extraordinary fuzzy ball, hanging against the silly background of blue sky, not unlike a visitor from another planet, saying: *Actually you are no one.*

In fact my racket has been on its way toward the ball for a whole chapter. The movement, which starts somewhere down to the right, has gone through all its phases, from right foot to left foot and back to the right again, the slow turn of the large dorsal muscles back and to the left and up again, the double strokes of the right arm through the still-cool morning air—all that was missing was a small turn of the wrist, the stroke itself. That's important in an American Twist, and without it the serve is easily transformed into a repulsive abortion which sails across the base line like a hot-air balloon.

It was a good serve. It hooked to the left according to plan and hit somewhere in the intersection between the corridor and the service line. I'd never have believed that the guy from STRATEGIC AIR FORCE HANDBALL TEAM whose name was Chris and who looked so damn nearsighted would have been able to hit it so far out, but he did.

He must have been a bit pressed anyhow, for his return shot was a little low. My partner at the net was in position. He hit a volley as clear as a small silver bell, and I was already on my way across to the next serve when something incredible happened.

THE BALL WAS ON ITS WAY BACK!

It was incomprehensible, but somehow that little girl had had time to get down to the corner of the net and even managed to hit a hard backhand. My half of the court was as open as a barn door, and I was completely out of countenance, since I had been interrupted in my quiet walk across to the advantage side to take care of the next serve.

I ran like hell to the right, arrived with my tongue hanging out, and hit a kind of half-volley. The situation started to get a bit tense. Volley again from that damn little girl, lightning swift return from my partner, new long backhand from Chris, this time down the line, but it went outside with about an inch to spare.

My second serve hit the net with a great big thud. If I make a really good serve the next one always hits the net. I've never had a second serve. I made much too short a serve, which was returned along the line like a streak of lightning. I didn't have a chance.

I'd already given up when, paralyzed, I became aware that my partner had taken it instead of me. He just appeared all of a sudden, and without actually running; with his incredible capacity for anticipation, he had simply walked there before Chris had even hit the ball.

He placed it in the ideal spot, right between our opponents. It gave me the uncomfortable feeling of not quite belonging.

"Excuse me," Abel said, pushing his leather hat back and wiping his eyes with his headband. The rims of his eyes were slightly inflamed as if he'd been staring into the sun for balls too often. "Excuse me, but it occurred to me that you might not be quite used to the placement."

"Oh," I said. "I'd never have made it."

Naturally my next serve was a double fault. The ball after that, I ruined it all by trying a smash that was much too deep. It was that damn girl again—she lobbed deliberately to see if I'd be able to return it, and then a lot of things happened that I've forgotten until I suddenly realized that the score was "ad out" and that it was about time I shaped up.

I always bounce the ball twice before I serve. Just as I was about to bounce it for the second time I happened to look up. I caught sight of some branches of the huge pecan behind me; a couple of twigs moved slightly in the morning breeze, and on the topmost twig a bird perched.

It made me feel happy. If you've eaten of Fafnir's heart you can understand the language of birds. What a shame there was no dragon to kill so that I could cut out his abominable black heart and make soup from it and finally know what the birds are singing, I thought. And for some reason, I put this whole thought into my serve.

It was a service ace. Dangerously close to the middle line, but a service ace just the same.

Abel gave me a searching look, from top to toe. I myself looked modestly at my shoes, for that's what you're supposed to do.

"Listen, I think you're *onto something*," he said.

Up by the net—it occurs to me now, long afterward, that it must have been a couple of games later on—I was supposed to pass the balls across to the girl named Polly. There were five of them.

Now something funny happened. When I handed the balls over, one by one, I noticed her hands. They were so warm. Or our hands were so warm together that we noticed it right away. For an incredible, brief moment we simply let go of all the balls and stood there holding hands across the net. I don't think anyone else had time to notice, it was that quick.

Three games later, when it was time to exchange balls once more, she carefully *threw* them across, one by one, impersonally, with unnecessary force in her throws.

The time was getting on for nine o'clock. It was already hot. We kept on playing. I have to confess that the tempo was a bit fast for me. Toward the end I could hardly keep track of either game points or side changes.

Nine o'clock on the dot everybody stopped as naturally as they had started and disappeared as anonymously as they had appeared. Polly threw herself into a huge old Dodge in which a wolfish German shepherd emerged from the back seat with a howl of enthusiasm. Evidently he'd been lying there waiting for her the whole time. She disappeared in a cloud of dust.

The man in the leather hat called Abel was the only one who didn't seem to be in a hurry.

"Listen, I guess I'll stay a while longer. There may be some other guys turning up who'll want to play."

I suddenly realized that in all probability, he spent all day on the tennis court. Surfers in California spend month after month at the same beach, doggedly waiting for the great, definitive wave, and similarly, there are a lot of people in Texas who spend their time on or beside tennis courts.

"Do you want to come along for a beer?" Chris asked. "It's getting hot, don't you think?"

"Sure thing," I said.

"I live right around here," he said.

He had the same kind of bike I did. We struggled up some steep hills and down some others and entered a leafy neighborhood of one-family houses.

The house was almost palatial in size; of course it had antiquated Colonial columns of painted wood. It stood on a high terrace. We followed a driveway in and biked practically into the kitchen.

Two workmen were standing on a stepladder, obviously smoking grass. In the kitchen a beautiful dark-haired lady was giving instructions to a blonde German maid, a medieval German girl like the ones in Albrecht Dürer drawings, in good German.

In the living room a rather heavy guy was teaching boxing to a boy about twelve. They were both wearing boxing gloves and were pulling the rugs out of place all the time as they side-stepped and ran around each other.

The painters, carpenters, or whatever they were, seemed to have serious difficulties getting the grass to light. They were using a pipe lined with foil.

"Come on," Chris said, "let's go up to my room. It's a bit disorganized around here this time of day."

"Is this your family," I asked.

"Family," he said. "We're not a family, exactly. Just some people living here. Actually only Professor Hobstone lives here. That dark-haired lady you saw. She's a psychiatrist. She wants to have some of her patients live with her for a while. I'm one of her patients myself, by the way."

I decided to ask no more familiar questions. The house must have had at least three floors; we climbed one stair after another, each steeper than the other.

"This is where I live," said Chris, opening the door.

It was a tower room, hexagonal, with lots of bookshelves and a real astronomical telescope, a Questar aimed at the balcony doors. On the floor, among piles of paper and books, was a typewriter. Other than that there was no furniture, just soft cushions.

"I don't like furniture," Chris said. "It makes me want to puke." He disappeared into a closet and emerged with two cans of ice-cold Dos XX's, an excellent Mexican beer. He must have had a refrigerator in the closet.

41

Lots of open notebooks, of the square-ruled type, full of complicated formulas, were thrown here and there. I moved one of them and a minicomputer of the very best kind, a Texas Instruments SR-51, so that I'd have a place to sit down.

I couldn't help looking at the notebook. The only thing I was able to understand was that several of the formulas contained a definite integral.

"Are you plotting planetary courses," I said jokingly.

"I tried to find one of Jupiter's moons last night. There was an article about it in *Scientific American* that said that it's probably the only place in our solar system where there's vegetation."

"Oh," I said, "I just read that article."

"I wasn't able to find it," said Chris, sadly putting his beer can down.

A cat slipped into the room so quietly that you weren't aware of it until it was already there. He took it into his arms and petted it with such childish tenderness that I realized he was only half an adult.

"I found the place where it was, but I didn't find the object itself. There's too much background light in the city."

"Too bad," I said.

The cat had started purring.

It was an unusually large cat, reddish colored, with long, elegant fur. To me, being from Västmanland, cats are always reminiscent of milking time in the barn.

"Are you an astronomer?" I asked, mostly so that I'd have something to say.

"No. I'm into cybernetics. When I was twelve my stepfather gave me one of Norbert Wiener's books. There was a place in it that fascinated the hell out of me: that's where Wiener explains cybernetically why the mongoose will always defeat the rattlesnake. Once I'd grasped that I was able to grasp everything else. I was into programming and computer language at an age when all the other guys were collecting stamps. I kept it up through college, and I kept it up in grad school. I think I can say that I know quite a bit about programming and computers.

"It's just that I was a bit too active in SDS in the early sixties. I was on the Berkeley campus, and I was stupid enough to use my own name instead of some pseudonym in too many underground newspapers. I landed on FBI lists and CIA lists, and since then I haven't managed to get a decent job in computers.

"Since I'm still into computers, one of my ideas is for a minicomputer model that'll be one of the best in the world because it's got such a phenomenal memory. I feel a bit hamstrung, you might say.

"Things haven't been that great the last few years. To tell you the truth, I had a complete nervous breakdown two years ago, and it was just lucky for me that Liz, that's Professor Hobstone, found me.

"Now I've even got a little job three afternoons a week where I have access to a terrific computer; I've got a terminal in front of me again. I can do calculations, I can program, I can copy mathematical structures again. And this house isn't a bad place. I've got people around when I need them, and they leave me alone when I need that."

He leaned back thoughtfully and lay down on the rug without letting go of the cat, who was still indolently allowing his stomach to be scratched.

One of the very few ornaments in the room was an old-fashioned wall clock—in my childhood, I'd seen hundreds just like it in the front rooms of farmhouses in my home district in northern Västmanland. This one must have come from some Scandinavian nineteenth-century immigrant to Texas, I thought. The old clock started striking: ten slow, melancholy strokes.

"What kind of job have you got right now?" I asked.

"Oh, it's a shit job, just routine, but it gives me access to one of the best computer terminals in Texas, and one that isn't used all that much. I have the watch three days a week at Strategic Air Command. I monitor the Southern Air Defense District's operations computer in Fort Worth."

"That's quite something," I said. "And they haven't got anything against people who are on CIA lists?"

"It's obvious you're a foreigner," Chris said. "You see, the CIA isn't all that popular with the Defense Department after Vietnam. Anyway, it's a good computer; it's supposed to keep track of all the air traffic in the district south of the Mississippi all the way down to the Canal Zone, where another command post takes over. It keeps track of every airplane that's moving, it knows what it is, and if it's something that can't be identified it locks rockets onto the target until some fatcats decide whether the plane should be shot down. That's what it does in peace time. But in case of nuclear war it's supposed to do a lot more things, and that means it has surplus capacity. I'd estimate that is uses eleven percent of its capacity—something like that—in peace time."

His nearsighted blue eyes carefully scrutinized the leaf shadows dancing on the ceiling. The clock had returned to its original slow ticking. For some reason I liked this room.

"The surplus capacity, that's what I use when I sit there; you might say that I tap a huge reservoir just a bit."

"But doesn't anyone notice?"

He looked at me, pleasantly surprised behind his huge lenses. Sometimes he reminded you of a kindly country schoolteacher.

"As early as the twenties, Kurt Gödel showed that it's possible to copy parameters that apply to the whole algebraic calculus on a small part of the arithmetical system. In theory, it's possible to copy any structure on any other structure as long as it's differentiated and has enough content to function as a picture. You can make a map of Texas from bread crumbs and you can picture Shakespeare's *Hamlet* as the product of indivisible numbers. As long as I use my own computer language there isn't a shadow of a possibility that someone who doesn't have access to that language will be able to distinguish what goes on in the machine normally from what I put into it."

"Listen, suppose you've got two books, pretty thick, pretty full of content, and if you've got reason to suspect that one section in each of the books deals with exactly the same events, it's just that they're being described by two different people, would it be possible to feed such material into the computer to sort out the correspondences?"

He frowned. The childish blue eyes became almost black. Only the cat's purring and the clock's ticking were audible in the room.

45

"I suspect that it's the kind of problem that looks very simple, ridiculously simple, when you give it a fast look and that turns out to be incredibly difficult, perhaps completely impossible, when you get into it some more. You see, the problem is knowing what kinds of *units* you've got. For instance, what counts as an event? It's exactly the same problem as what elements of language carry meaning. Is it letters? Is it words? Is it phrases? Is it clauses? Or some still larger units? And isn't it possible to find certain events in every narrative that correspond to every other narrative? Man, you're getting in over your head if you start in on this. Anyway, what *kind* of stories are you talking about?"

"Hey there," someone shouts from below the labyrinth of stairs. "Chris. Lunch. Is that guy with the beard staying for lunch?"

"Do you want to?" Chris asked. "You're welcome to, but there's usually nothing much in the middle of the week."

It was a very noisy, disorderly, and merry lunch which we consumed in the middle of a dining room apparently in the process of receiving the ministrations of the two workmen. The kind of drop cloths used for painting hung everywhere. It turned out there were four children, two of them hefty numbers from the school football team, who ate quickly and greedily, and two rather small children, a brother and sister, who pelted each other with corn kernels through most of the meal; the German maid—she really was very beautiful—and her boyfriend, who apparently lived in the house and who made a rather pale, strikingly well-brought-up impression. Then there were the two workmen, who did not seem unaffected by having smoked grass all morning. And then, if I remember correctly, there was a small, quite fat, evidently unhappy dark-haired little number at the foot of the table who persisted, God knows why, in asking me questions about Igor Stravinsky. Did she take me for a Russian?

Professor Liz seemed to be one of those rare female saints you run across, if you're on the move a lot, once or twice in your life. She seemed to be sufficient unto them all.

The girl at the foot of the table was just shouting something to me about Stravinsky's *Symphony of Psalms*, her cheeks full of corn kernels, when Chris leaned close to me and said, quietly but not so quietly that all the others couldn't hear it too:

"Listen, Lars."

"Mmm."

"You've never been to one of the Strategic Air Command Operations Centers, have you?"

"No, somehow I never have," I said. "That kind of place is totally outside my normal sphere of activity."

"Tomorrow I'm driving over to Fort Worth early, and I'm going to work there in the afternoon. You can come along if you'd like, and bring those two books in some intelligible language. English, for instance. We can give it some thought at any rate."

"That'd really be great. But are you sure they'll let me in?"

"Why not?"

"Well, I don't know. They might think I was a Russian or something."

"Russian, good lord, did you say *Russian*? We've got

47

study groups from the Frunze Academy coming in every week or so. There's nothing they like better than showing it to Russians. You see, the Russians are so terribly impressed each time. Why don't you get over here by half past six. It'll take us at least three and a half hours to drive there because of the heavy traffic."

"Great, fantastic," I said. "Just great. I don't have any classes tomorrow."

After lunch Chris, in spite of violent protests from the Stravinsky girl, insisted on putting Wagner's *Götterdämmerung* on a rather loud stereo in the living room. He told me that he loved Wagner and especially *Götterdämmerung*.

"That fits in well with your job," I said, escaping on my bike. I had a few things to do that day, and already I was quite a bit behind.

5. *Götterdämmerung*: Act One

Oh, those sunrises in Texas! I'll never forget them.

At that time I often fooled around with a novel I was writing, and I used to get up as early as half past five and sit at the kitchen table with a large cup of bitter coffee, watching the sun rise, while one of the local radio stations played loud classical music.

The spectacle was always equally impressive. The whole eastern part of the sky seemed filled with groping fingers of rose and violet before the awesome, glowing white orb triumphantly broke through the line of the horizon.

It must have had some connection with the vast deserts, or perhaps with the dust clouds, or with the humidity from the perpetually moist air over the Gulf of Mexico; the fact is that I've never seen the likes of it anywhere.

The only thing I can compare it to is the place in *Das Rheingold* by Richard Wagner where the stage directions say: "A still lighter brilliance has penetrated the water in the river. In a high place on the middle reef it finally erupts into a golden flame from which blinding rays shoot out; an enchanting golden light suffuses the water."

I would sit, quite empty and quite happy, looking out at the eastern horizon before it was time to brush my teeth and then sit for a few hours dreaming over my typewriter, describing a hero who had lost his way in the bureaucratic labyrinth of 1960s Sweden. This hero had certain intimate characteristics in common with me, and the grislier the the narrative got, the better I felt in the peaceful Texas winter morning.

It was the same kind of enjoyment as when you're lying in your warm bed on a rainy autumn night, reading about a horseman riding through the icy rain to carry an important message to some distant duke.

The more difficult things got for the protagonist of my novel in his winter-dark, tangled, and increasingly incomprehensible and frightening Sweden, the calmer and more idyllic I felt in my dry, clear Texas morning.

Now this was a particular morning, one that parted the idyllic curtain somewhat, but I didn't know that at the time.

I pulled on my jeans, threw my shirt on top, and made a couple of sandwiches in case of emergency, tossed them into my backpack together with a notebook and an ID that gave me access to all the gym and sports events at the whole university. Soon I was on my way up the hills, using the highest gear, so fast that my bike creaked.

Chris was already sitting in his car, honking impatiently, sleepy and rather taciturn.

Soon we were outside the district of green hills and fresh lakes which comprise Travis County. The landscape flattened around us, the plain became endless and reddish; here and there a lonely derrick plunged up and down in some oil-producing district, surrounded by grazing longhorns. The further out we came, the more the traffic slackened. As always, I felt an indistinct awe before the immense, seemingly boundless dimensions of the Texas landscape.

You always felt like Euclid, made to measure Hades with a pair of compasses and a ruler, on these endless plains. They could give you a feeling of confinement, as intensely as the Berlin wall does. Only in quite a different way, of course.

After two hours we stopped in Waxahachie and bought a couple of hot dogs and some coffee. I was stiff from sitting so long in the car. I simply wasn't used to it.

After another forty-five minutes we left the main road and turned down a side road which, after just half an hour, turned into something like a farm road, dusty and narrow, meandering across sparse grazing land in the direction of a gigantic barbed-wire fence.

"Well, this is my moonlighting job," Chris said.

"I thought it was in Fort Worth," I said.

"No," Chris said, "the city's down there to the west. Sometimes after dark you can see it lighting up the sky."

I glimpsed some kind of low barracks half a mile or so beyond the fence. That was all. And some kind of small guardhouse next to the gate, the kind you see at a lot of plants nowadays. If the guard hadn't been carrying an M16 and holding back two huge German shepherds who jumped about and strained at the leash, you might have imagined yourself at the gates of a mine in Västmanland. Chris slowed down and waved his ID through the car window. That helped right away. The gates opened on electric hinges, and I had a slight feeling of unreality, an unpleasant feeling of not having been taken seriously that always hits me on the rare occasions when I manage to get across a border or through a police barrier without being selected for some special kind of control.

Deep inside I know that I'm one of the most dangerous criminals in Europe. It's just that I haven't quite got started on my criminal activities. So far.

It was the quietest, most desolate place in the world. Some turkey vultures hung over the place—for some reason, Texas was full of vultures that winter—but otherwise nothing but those low buildings. Not even a telephone wire disturbed the peace.

In one of those buildings, we went down in an elevator for at least four minutes, and when we stepped out on a floor which, judging by its number, was at least one hundred and fifty feet below ground, there were suddenly crowds of people passing through the corridors. Some of them were in uniform, some in white coats, and some, like Chris, in jeans and shirts.

We walked straight ahead through a huge corridor, passed a whole lot of people, among them some good-looking girls gathered around a coffee machine, and turned sharply to the left. To my amazement we entered another elevator, one of those that don't have buttons and that you have to operate with a key. After a lot of trouble, Chris found a Yale key in the narrow back pocket of his jeans and put it into the keyhole; the elevator door closed without a sound.

This time we went straight down without passing any floors, damn far down and so fast that my stomach pressed against my diaphragm.

ZONE A it said on the concrete wall. Chris pressed a button and spoke into a microphone. Suddenly a narrow door slid open.

The room we entered may have been very large, but it was so faintly illuminated by weak, dotlike lights and terminal screens which shimmered bluish white that it was impossible to see the walls.

A strikingly pale and thin, very tall guy with a crewcut

52

and a clipboard-type notebook emerged from the semi-darkness.

"Hi there," he said to Chris.

"This is it," Chris whispered in my right ear, stepping toward him jauntily.

"Hi. This is Professor Gustafsson from Austin."

I showed him my teeth in a magnificent Texas grin.

"Hi," I said, "What's the situation? Any problems?"

He gave me a serious look.

"The random access memory still acts up from time to time." I whistled.

"Damn! I'll have a look at it. Are you sure you're adhering to standard procedure?"

He looked at me as if I'd insulted his mother.

"Of course you are," I said, giving my gold-rimmed glasses a careful polish. I looked deeply into his pale blue eyes, not unlike two aquariums exactly the same size, without fish of course, and said with the force of total sincerity:

"I've no *idea* what it could be. But I'll have a look just the same."

Chris and the thin guy went to one side, spoke softly and laughed. It seemed the pale guy was telling Chris about someone who'd fucked up that morning, or was he talking about a girl on the switchboard?

They talked and laughed with each other for such a long time that I almost started to think they were a bit impolite. Then he quickly handed his notes to Chris, who checked something off nearsightedly.

The pale guy disappeared.

The air conditioning hissed softly. Chris signaled to me to follow him through a green door.

This was evidently where the monster had been set up. An endless row of lamps that flickered and died, magnetic memory tapes rolling back and forth inside protective glass shields, writing terminals and screens.

Chris let his hand play across a row of switches, and a huge screen in the ceiling lit up—or rather it was a screen suspended at an angle from the ceiling. It took a moment before I understood that the different lines, glowing in different shades of green, represented a map of an immense district. It was easy to recognize Texas with its Panhandle to the north, the wide arch of Rio Grande to the south, and then Mexico and Central America, all the way down to Ecuador.

All over this strange green picture little white pinpoints of light moved, occasionally thickening to swarms. Almost every dot was accompanied on its way across the map by some kind of formula, a series of letters with a couple of figures.

"This is what it looks like. Fun, isn't it? It's the airspace above Texas, and this computer keeps track of all of it. Take that dot on its way from Dallas out over the Atlantic, for instance. It's the lunch flight for Frankfurt; it's just climbed to thirty thousand feet. In a little while it'll get up to forty thousand, and there it'll stay, and then it'll disappear out of our district. Then the Early Distant Warning System in Alaska will take over."

"Incredible swarm over Dallas," I said.

"It's the largest airport in the world."

"What's that red thing off the Gulf of Mexico?"

"An atomic submarine. It hasn't moved much since yesterday."

"What happens if anything *foreign* gets in?"

"Lots of things. If it's a single plane traveling at normal speed, first of all one of the guys out there contacts it and asks what it is. But the computer locks a weapon onto him right away. Look here: I can program in a foreign plane if I want to."

"Don't do that, for heaven's sake."

"Ah, I'll take it off again so fast that nothing'll happen. This terminal isn't the big terminal: I can free it any time I want to."

He did some typing on one of the machines and pointed up at the screen. "Now there should be an unidentified dot there"—he pointed south of the Gulf of Mexico—"a plane heading toward Washington at a speed of twelve thousand miles an hour, at an altitude of seventy-five thousand feet."

Suddenly the white dot assumed a bright red color and started blinking. It moved slowly, like a minute hand, but it did move.

"Now watch closely."

Suddenly a red ring flamed up around the blinking dot.

"If the computer hadn't been on simulator, the weapons system would have locked its radar antennae on it right now."

"Then what would happen?"

"The concrete covers would slide open in some bunker somewhere and a Minuteman would take off in a cloud of fire and smoke."

"Are you quite sure that this doesn't go into the real Operations System?" I asked.

"Quite sure. Look at this switch."

"Yes."

"If I throw it it becomes reality. Then this information is fed into the national system. Sometimes I play a fun game here. I call it 'playing *Götterdämmerung*.'"

"Good lord," I said.

"I'll program about eight hundred very fast planes in perfect formation coming on over the coast, and when the computer has absorbed it all—it takes several seconds—I'll erase everything again."

"What happens if you throw that switch instead?"

"I don't know. Maybe nothing. There are master computers that get no information from anywhere else. Probably it would go as far as a lot of planes taking off and a lot of concrete covers sliding open. As I said, I really don't know. But it's a funny feeling. Perhaps it would be possible to wipe out the whole human race from here. What do you think?"

I felt a bit uneasy but didn't want to show it.

"Of course it would be possible. You can wipe out the whole human race if you take a large whiskey and go to bed," I said. "A much cheaper method, above all much more humane."

To my relief he had taken off the foreign plane. Evidently we were plugged into the large network once more. There seemed to be a lot of activity at low altitude around the Austin Airport.

"It's the ranchers in their planes going to the football game in Waco. Today's Friday."

He turned off the large picture again. Only the small terminal screen glowed in front of us.

"Have you ever considered what a *superfluous* gismo this whole death machine is," Chris said. "Everybody dies anyway, without the help of bunkers, rockets, game plans, computers."

"But not simultaneously," I said. "I asume that what you're paying for is simultaneity. Let's ask the computer something," I added, having a feeling that it was time to change the topic. I sat down in front of the terminal.

"What do you want to ask?"

"How many different ways can forty-three people make love?"

"Two and two," Chris asked.

"Yes."

"Without consideration as to sex."

"Yes."

"A ridiculously simple problem."

"180̸6," the computer said, cocksure.

"And if you separate the sexes?"

"How many are women?"

"Half."

"That won't work."

"Why not?"

"Half of forty-three makes twenty-one point five."

I wrote into the computer, "DO̸ES EVIL EXIST?"

"What do you think yourself?" Chris asked.

"I don't know. Well, yes, I believe it does exist."

"INSTRUCTIO̸N INCO̸MPLETE," the machine remarked discreetly.

"STO̸RE QUESTIO̸N MEMO̸RY 12," Chris vengefully tapped back on the keyboard.

"YO̸U ARE A BLO̸O̸DY KILLER," I wrote.

"INSTRUCTIO̸N INCO̸MPLETE," answered the servile machine.

"STO̸RE INSTRUCTIO̸N MEMO̸RY 3," I added on the sly.

"SIGNATURE," the machine blinked angrily at me.

"He wants to know who's programming this memory.

57

You've got to have a series of numbers that shows you've got the right to enter Memory 3. That's one of its best memories."

"GØD," I wrote.

"SIGNATURE UNSATISFACTØRY," the machine challenged me.

"SHUT UP YØU BLØØDY MØTHERFUCKER," I wrote.

Strangely enough it did. Right away.

I dug *Inferno* and *Memoires d'un chimiste* out of my coat pockets.

"You can't do a damn thing about them in here," I said.

Chris looked up at me. His eyes looked abnormally large behind the convex lenses.

"Let me read them anyway," he said. "It's boring just to sit here. At least they'll be a help, so I don't invent too many new games." He gave me an ironic look.

With a sigh he leaned across the list of routine checks. His afternoon had begun.

The illuminated map of the Southern Air Defense District again dominated the scene. A thousand little white dots on their way to and from places, through jet streams, over and under mighty cloud banks at every altitude between ninety thousand feet and nine hundred, dominated the afternoon.

It was raining buckets when I got back home around ten in the evening, one of those powerful Texas downpours which make it seem that the water is being poured out in large tepid pailfuls from above.

My apartment smelled close. A trace of the heat of the

day was left in the room but with a hint of something unpleasant, sour.

There's algae in the air-conditioning system again.

The telephone rang violently just as I was about to sit down in front of the TV.

It was Doobie, of all people. She was overjoyed.

"I've got a job," she shouted. "I'll be getting some money."

"That's great. What are you going to do?"

"Flosshilde."

"Excuse me?"

"Flosshilde. You mean you really don't know who Flosshilde is?"

I leaned out through the open window. The rain was streaming down like a waterfall; in the distance, huge flashes of lightning illuminated the night and made the telephone poles in the street throw long, strangely shaped shadows.

It smelled of damp fall earth, of ozone, and of rich red mud.

"Which damn Flosshilde?" I asked.

"Flosshilde is one of the Rhine Maidens, you know. She's the one who's a mezzo. They're going to stage *Das Rheingold* at the Stadium on January twentieth. With Vico Varossi from Milan as director, and the student orchestra and all the singers will be from the university. Extremely lavish. I had an audition with Varossi yesterday."

"Well?"

"Very nice guy. Don't you understand what this means? I'll have money again. We'll both manage, my sister and I, the whole spring semester. There's just one catch."

"What?"

"Never mind, I'll tell you when I see you."

I left the window open; the rain kept streaming down the same way hour after hour, and in my dreams I thought it was a flood. Somehow I had got *Das Rheingold* and *Die Götterdämmerung* confused. The whole world was under water, and the Rhine Maidens were floating around between the houses in fantastic green bathing suits, and Chris turned up in the middle of this aquarium world, and his eyes were related to the aquarium eyes of that pale guy down by the Defense Operations machine, and he said threateningly:

"If you don't tell me your secret, I'll pull out the plug."

"Is there a plug you can pull out?" I asked.

"Of course there is," he said.

In the morning it was clear and warm once more. I decided to take another look at the tennis courts.

6. Nietzsche against Wagner, Abel against Connors, Elephant against Donkey, Everybody against Everybody

Down in the park, it was an unusually quiet morning. Fred, an elderly man with Bismarck features, was setting up his vegetable stand. He looked so much like the Iron Chancellor that one might have been mistaken for the other were it not for the fact that Fred wore a large white apron across his stomach.

The court, still wet in spots after the night's rain, at first seemed quite empty. I leaned my bike carefully against the chicken wire; when I bent to chain it with the steel cable a rhythmic singing started in the wire.

I looked up and discovered Abel, still alone with his funny, wide-brimmed leather hat. With terrifying monotony he was hitting a ball against the other fence, from a very short distance, forehands all the time.

"Hello there," I said.

He caught the ball deftly in his hand and turned around leisurely.

"Oh, it's you," he said.

He seemed somehow preoccupied or distraught. Without further comment we went to opposite ends of the court. He sent me a ball with a strong topspin, far down toward the base line. I didn't think it quite polite to start a warm-up ball like that: it seemed snooty somehow. I felt a brief aggressive impulse.

To my surprise this impulse translated itself into an excellent forehand. Not just anybody could have hit it back. Abel got to it and returned a backhand with topspin. I tried placing it to one side, mostly to tease him, but the ball had secret stores of charged power. The only thing I could do was to hit it very hard into the net, where it hung like a ridiculous caught fish.

"Serve a couple of balls to me," I said.

He served five. I wasn't able to return a single one. The balls looked like slightly squashed eggs on their way toward me. The only one I had any kind of control over I hit into the net.

"Your serve is worse than Connors'," I shouted.

"No, that isn't true," he shouted back angrily.

"How do you know?"

"I played against him a couple of years ago at Forest Hills and lost."

The remark paralyzed me. During the next five minutes I performed a miraculous series of five double faults.

"I don't want to play today, I'm not in good form," I said.

"Nonsense. You're just trying to make yourself small so you won't lose," he said. "You want to deprive me of the chance to beat you, you want to do it yourself. Drop it. Let's play and see what happens instead."

That turned out to be a pretty good idea. I held my serve for two games and lost 2–6. There are sets I've won 6–0 that I'm less proud of. There was something in his play, aggressively confident and brilliant, which got strokes out of me that I'd never have believed myself capable of. The most amusing moment was a high backhand volley that actually rendered him defenseless. Of course I missed the next ball completely, turning it into a looping lob. It returned as a smash which made the wire ring like a cymbal.

"That's enough," I said after one set. "This isn't really my tempo, my level."

"You weren't bad," Abel said calmly. "It's just that I'm very good."

"Can you tell me something," I said.

"I suspected that you'd ask about that, many people do. I've played at Forest Hills, I've participated in the WCT tournament, I've won the Australian Open once, and I've come in second at Wimbledon twice. But I prefer to play here with people who come by."

"Why?"

"Because it's more *fun*. Because I don't feel like it any longer. There's nothing strange or tragic about it. It's just that I've stopped. I'm no longer a *pro*."

"Just like the surfers in California who used to be dentists and electronic engineers and all kinds of things and suddenly end up living by the beach waiting for a wave," I said.

"You got me," he said. "By the way, you should give more thought to your thumb."

"What do you mean," I asked.

"You hold it a little too horizontal for a Western Grip."

"How in the world can you see that at such a distance?"

"I don't see it. I hear it from the sound—something else, too."

"Yes?"

He seemed to hesitate, as if the revelation he was about to make was too horrible.

"Never think about the ball that's gone. It's gone, whether it was good or bad it's gone just the same. There's never any ball except the one you've got in front of you."

On the stroke of ten I entered the seminar room. The flies were buzzing on the ceiling more aggressively than ever; the students were as incomprehensibly sleepy as ever. What on earth are those students up to at night, *don't they ever get to bed*, I thought.

"Now for the seventh time," I said. "What do you suppose Nietzsche means in his massive attack on the composer, *The Wagner Case*, when he says, 'Now the musician becomes an actor; his art develops more and more into a talent for *lying*'?"

An emptiness like that of the desert by the Rio Grande echoed from the room. I went to look out the window. A row of black limousines proudly rolled up in front of the main building with the library tower.

Out of the first stepped Mr. Hugh Frisco, Commissioner of Cultural Affairs, Chairman of the Board of Trustees, a nutcracker face in a chalk-striped suit. Out of the next one emerged Geoffrey Gore, oil millionaire, Honorary Doctor of Engineering, local Republican bigshot.

There was an involved system of parking regulations at the university, determined by different-colored windshield stickers. The students, furthest away, miles from campus; the research assistants, a bit closer; associate professors and full professors, still closer. But in front of the sacred main building, in front of the tower, only ten people in the whole world were allowed to park, the ten possessors of gold stickers that showed the car's owner was a member of the Board of Trustees.

"Good lord," I said to my class. "What day of the week is this?"

"Wednesday," six or seven merry voices answered at the same time.

64

"Then there are big things afoot. The Board of Trustees meet on Fridays. Now the whole gang's here. You can bet anything that they're going to fire the president of the university again."

The university was known all over the United States for its incredible, always dramatic and sudden firings of its presidents. During the past three years, four presidents had come and gone. A continual battle was being waged among a bunch of oil magnates, gangster lawyers, and local politicians, who more or less regarded the university as their private property, and a collection of progressively paler and more frightened presidents. The first one to be fired, four years ago, was a world-renowned liberal arts scholar. The present incumbent was a kindly, rotund professor of forestry, John R. Perturber, Jr.

Normally the ceremony would consist of the members of the board marching into the president's magnificent office, presenting him with his own letter of resignation to sign.

I've been told that as late as the 1920s, the trustees would also place a revolver on his desk.

The clock in the tower struck eleven. The students and I were still staring out the window. On the lawn outside students were not stretched out in graceful groups on the grass. They stood up to watch.

The last three presidential firings had all led to violent demonstrations.

"You may leave now," I said. "But for next week, give some thought to this: *Now the musician becomes an actor; his art develops more and more into a talent for lying.* In that statement, one of the profound secrets of the nineteenth century lies hidden."

"But this isn't the nineteenth century," said a small

65

defiant guy named Hank. Hank Norton, if I remember correctly.

Today he was wearing a funny kind of shirt. Frankenstein's Monster adorned its front like some kind of emblem.

I often thought that the students in my undergraduate seminar were more fun than the ones in the graduate seminar. We seemed to play better together.

I left the classroom loaded with books, went into the secretaries' room, and dropped them all on the floor as I tried to get some coffee from the machine. I got my mail, which consisted of a somewhat delapidated copy of *Expressen* and a letter from a lecture club in Köping back in Sweden whose chairman stated that for the last few weeks he had tried unsuccessfully to get me on the phone.

"There's a Board meeting," I said to Peggy, our secretary. She nodded.

"I've noticed."

"What's happening?"

"The dean's just trying to find out. He's calling the other deans."

I sat down in front of the desk in my office. Outside my window the sprinklers whirled across the emerald-green lawns. There were still a couple of hours until lunchtime.

I put my chin on my crossed arms on the desk top. The books that covered the desk were transformed into a strange kind of cityscape with streets and alleys. Benedetto Croce's *Storia d'Europa nel seculo decimono* lay at an angle between Ibsen streets in a way that reminded me of the Anglais building at Stureplan in Stockholm.

66

Down Kungsgatan crawled a large, reddish, very exotic Texas ant; he crossed the street and turned by *Jenseits von Gut and Böse* to enter Stureplan, hesitated there for a moment, gobbled up some bread crumbs left from my afternoon coffee break two days ago, and then he disappeared at a good clip up toward Humlegården along the imposing façades formed by Fritz Mauthner's *Beiträge zu einer Kritik der Sprache.*

I wondered if perhaps there were more ants like that in my office and if they constituted a danger to my manuscripts. Some years earlier, the whole institution had been plagued by laboratory rats that had escaped from the psychologists in the cellar along the antiquated ventilation ducts and had then got into a most humanistic atmosphere. It's a fact that American psychology uses up quite a few rats and mice.

I was torn from my reverie by the angry ringing of my phone. It was Chris. His voice sounded distant. There was a buzzing on the line, or perhaps there was a buzzing in the room where he was speaking. I can't pretend my happiness at hearing from him was unmitigated. The trip to the desert outside of Fort Worth had scared me somewhat. Just how crazy was he? Did he really have the chance to start World War III? And was it actually consonant with advanced theories of psychotherapy to rehabilitate people by giving them access to machinery that governed armed nuclear warheads in gigantic rockets hidden one hundred and fifty feet underground in concrete bunkers? I had seriously considered calling Professor Hobstone after that trip, but the thought of lifting the receiver didn't exactly appeal to me. I kept procrastinating.

Anyway, could it be considered consonant with modern psychiatry to build gigantic nuclear rockets into underground bunkers and allow them to be governed by suspect electronic brains far under the earth? In fact, was Chris any crazier than anyone else in Fort Worth?

"Hi," Chris said. "I've coded those two books now, by optic reading. It took all night, and my fingers are sore from turning the pages. This morning the machine is Gödel-numbering the whole thing. It'll probably take about twenty hours before it's finished, but there are great advantages. I can transfer a lot of memory capacity so it isn't so easy to discover that the machine is moonlighting."

"Excuse me, but what do you mean by Gödel-numbering?"

"Sorry, I can't hear you very well, all the writing units are going full speed."

"HOW DO YOU MAKE A GÖDEL NUMBER?"

What? Oh yes. You mean you don't know. You number all the letters in the alphabet and all the punctuation marks, and then there's a special number for spaces between words. Then you take the product of those numbers for each sentence. And then you take the prime numbers and raise them to those products so that they're powers of the prime numbers. Since all prime numbers are unequivocally determined by their prime factors, you've tagged each sentence in a way that can never be lost. Then all you do is multiply the Gödel numbers of the sentences with one another, and that way you get the Gödel number for the whole book."

"Then they must be rather *large* numbers?"

"That's true. But when I'm finished all I've got is two

large numbers in the machine's memory, and I can throw away a couple of miles of magnetic tape, and then we can really get started. Let's see if we can't find some fun correlations between those two quantities."

"Sounds like fun, all right. And then what do you get?"

"No idea. Oh yes, of course there'll be a third book. *The Third Book* about the Inferno. It's possible to . . ."

There was a squeak in the receiver. I could hear voices in the background, metallic military voices.

"Listen, I've got to hang up now. I'll call you later. There's some kind of *alert* here."

Not particularly reassured, I hung up. Since the sun was still shining from a thin blue winter sky, since the sprinklers still spread their rainbow shimmer peacefully across the lawn, and since Doobie had just limped in through the door, I assumed that World War III was not imminent.

Doobie always limped a little when she was perfectly furious. It was one of her peculiarities. She had been in a highway accident as a child. The only consequence seemed to be that she limped when she was excited.

"How are you? What's up?" I asked. "Do you know what a *Gödel number* is?"

"Number-schmumber," Doobie answered. "*God.* I've got to sit down."

She speedily removed a sizable stack of books from my one and only visitor's chair.

"But Doobie dear," I said.

I'll cut his throat," Doobie sobbed.

"*Whose* throat?"

"Vico Varossi from Milan, of course."

"Why?"

"You should be able to figure that one out for yourself."

"The Maestro has become enamored of you."

"Exactly."

"And there's no Flosshilde part in *Das Rheingold* unless you grant him your favors, or whatever it's called?"

"Exactly."

"And that would be a fate worse than death?"

"He smells of garlic ten feet off."

"I understand. Wouldn't it be possible to interest him in one of the other Rhine Maidens? What does he think about Wellgunde? Has Woglinde no charm?"

"You're just making a joke of it. This is quite serious. It means I won't be getting any money for the rest of the semester."

"A damn shame. By the way, don't you have a contract?"

"I'm just an amateur. He can always say that I'm not up to the part, musically speaking."

"And are you?"

She looked at me with such a cruel, Lou Salomé kind of expression that I refrained from asking any more questions on that score.

I thought for a while.

"What does the Maestro look like? Does he seem very strong?"

"Ah, he's just a skinny little Italian who jumps up and down like a rubber ball when he's conducting."

"O.K.," I said. "I'll go talk to him after lunch. Where do you rehearse?"

70

"Wood's Gymnasium, in the big basketball court."

"Fine," I said. "I'll explain to him that we don't make a habit of *seducing our students* at this university. It goes against our traditions. And still less do we practice sexual blackmail on them. As long as he's connected with the College of Music he must be regarded as faculty. He comes under the University Statutes."

She left.

I was just looking around for my copy of the University Statutes when there was a knock on the door.

"*Come in*," I bellowed.

This day, which had started well, seemed to be getting difficult. I didn't like it.

The professor of Old Norse, my old friend John Weinstock, entered. He was in such a hurry that his long Texas mustache flapped in the wind, and a long black cigar was hanging unlit from his mouth.

He said in Norwegian, "Excuse me, but I've got to talk to you, Lars. Now they've fired the president again, and we have to discuss whether this department should go on strike."

"*Good lord*," I said.

Unsettling rumors flew across campus. Groups of students and faculty were standing talking to each other. From the business street west of the university grounds where, at this time of day, the small lunch places were usually filled with students and faculty, people were streaming in the opposite direction, onto campus. The University Police, graying country sheriffs who'd normally busy themselves with ticketing parking violators on the large grounds, seemed threateningly numerous.

71

The black limousines were still parked ominously in front of the main building.

Rumors and counterrumors crossed each other; the department telephones were red-hot from attempts to establish what exactly was happening in the board room with its crystal chandeliers and ankle-deep wall-to-wall carpeting.

This much was clear: Messrs. Frisco and Gore had presented some kind of ultimatum to the president, and the president had locked himself in his office and refused to answer this ultimatum until he'd had a conference with the deans. Once in his office he had found that his telephone didn't work any longer, and for about an hour the situation had remained stable; while the president sat locked in his office waiting for something to happen, the chairman and the oil magnate sat under the crystal chandeliers in the board room, also waiting for something to happen. It was the calm before the storm, so to speak.

The old gangster trick of cutting off the president's telephone lines was not particularly successful, since it effectively prevented anybody from doing anything whatsoever. And since no one knew what the ultimatum was, there wasn't even an ultimatum to demonstrate against. The student organizations, from the Trotskyites to the Daughters of the American Revolution, collected compact crowds around their booths, but as yet there were no protest lists to sign, and there were no slogans to write on the banners. One guy with a huge beard crept across the sidewalk and lettered OUR UNIVERSITIES ARE OCCUPIED on a four-man banner. A small black-haired girl was running around in the crowd, quick as a weasel, trying to distribute flyers which, to the obvious annoyance of the recipients, stated that Jesus had the solution to the problem.

The department meeting was brief. This was partly due to the fact that it was too soon to take action and partly to the fact that after four firings, everybody except me was used to it. *The thing to do was to keep in touch with the English Department*—that's about what I got out of it. It seemed the English Department played approximately the same role in this battle as Napoleon's artillery at Austerlitz.

I squeezed through the crowd, avoided three people I knew, and made my way through locker room passages and saunas and through teams of sweaty handball players to the basketball court on the third floor of Wood's Gymnasium.

I opened the door gingerly. Mighty orchestral sounds, strange dissonances with reduced fifths greeted me like warm air. The large room was faintly lit: the only illumination was the lights on the music stands and the makeshift working light on the stage. The Valhalla Motif surged out into the room with mild, seductive warmth, modulated to the Motif of Compact through three brilliant sixths, touched on the Siegfried Motif, by means of a solitary horn, for one giddy moment, and was superseded by the exquisite Motif of Eternal Youth. And then there was a shower of words.

"No, no, no, *not* so. *Il corno* you cannot play him so, not *come una tromba*. Wagner is *not* Gershwin, Wagner is *not* film music. Wagner was a *revolutionary*. Who do we find on the Dresden barricades in 1830? *Wagner!* Yeeees, naturally, Richard Wagner, Bakunin's friend. Siegfried is an *anarchista*, the whole *Ring* she is about

73

this, that the laws do *not* apply, that the gods even must fall. Is it *not* called *The Twilight of the Gods*? Alberich and Mime who destroy the gold, that is *industrialismo. Capito? Capitalismo contra natura, si.* The horn must be played in quite a different way, *come anarchista. Capito? Così*: Da-daaa-da, da-daa.—*Much bedder*!

The man on the podium looked like a musician straight out of the *Tales* of E.T.A. Hoffman.

Doobie had described him as small and thin; he was that, but in exactly the same way in which a lizard is small and thin. Pale, with a fanatical glow in his eyes, amazingly like those fanatical conductors and violinists who fill the early nineteenth century with their strange stories of contracts with the devil and peculiar black-coated gentlemen in hansom cabs who commission orchestral works from them for immense sums and on strange conditions. He climbed up and down on the podium, swung from the orchestra pit onto the stage with the aid of a contrabassoonist's chair, down into the pit again, nervously leafing through the first violinist's music.

Probably he was enveloped in a cloud of garlic. I was too far away to notice.

I was considering how to find a suitable pause in the rehearsal to go up to the podium and get his attention. Perhaps they'd take a coffee break some time?

Wotan and Loge were having a confab on stage with the conductor. Freia, in a very tight sweater, lay prone on the stage floor and seemed to be doing isometric exercises. From the standing-room balcony, where I was, it was impossible to tell whether she was beautiful or ugly, but her breasts looked immense.

Then they ran through the orchestral part. Just as the

74

horn player was about to make his anarchistic contribution, some guy came running up the center aisle to the podium and started shouting for all he was worth to get the conductor's attention.

That wasn't the easiest thing in the world. When the conductor noticed him at last, he at first looked as if he seriously considered hitting him with his baton.

The young man who'd come in was waving a piece of paper.

When he'd waved it long enough the conductor snatched it. I think at first he intended to tear it into little pieces, but something on the paper must have caught his attention.

He didn't turn the orchestra off. One group of instruments after another fell silent as the musicians gradually realized that something out of the ordinary had occurred. Scattered clarinets, an oboe, and an English horn continued to play their parts passionately, long after the others had stopped. The whole thing made an unpleasant impression of entropy, regression, paralysis. It was as if the music had died under our ears.

Now several musicians climbed out of the pit and gathered around the podium.

The Maestro read the note over and over. It didn't seem to tell him very much; he seemed to have a hard time making friends with it. He turned it every which way; I'm damned if he didn't actually hold it upside down at one point.

He waved the note angrily. More and more musicians and singers gathered around him. I climbed down carefully from one row of seats to the next and joined the quickly thickening crowd.

"I understand *nothing*. It is nonsense. Verdi! elephants!

Academic program! Academic freedom! This is *madness*! *Porca miseria!*"

The first bassoonist, a profusely freckled guy with whom I had once played tennis, by the way, was the only one to keep his cool. He climbed up beside the Maestro on the podium and simply took the piece of paper from him. His forehead creased too.

Scattered shouts of impatience were heard from the audience.

The first bassoonist seemed to be something of a diva and had to be coaxed. Eventually, he cleared his throat and read:

"The Board of Trustees of this university have today, through Hugh Frisco, Doctor of Law (Hon. Caus.), relayed an ultimatum to me. If I do not submit my resignation as President Magnificus of this university, due to poor health, before six P.M., I will be fired, effective immediately.

"In the course of my conversations with delegates from the Board of Trustees, it has become apparent that an important reason for this stand is that I, contrary to the express wishes of Mr. Gore and Mr. Frisco that the Spring Concert should be a performance of Guiseppe Verdi's opera *Aida*, with live elephants on stage in the victory scene, have given my permission, in accordance with the express wishes of the orchestra and the choir, for a performance of the German composer Richard Wagner's opera *Das Rheingold*.

"The spokesmen have insisted that, partly out of consideration for the well-known Democratic traditions of the German-speaking population of Travis County, partly because the elephant is the traditional symbol of

76

the Republican party, my decision with regard to the choice of Spring Opera constitutes a political statement.

"I have refused to accept this ultimatum, which I construe as an attempt at political interference with the academic program at this university. I appeal to faculty and students to give me their support in this difficult situation.

(signed) John R. Perturber, Jr."

A shout of anger rose from orchestra and singers. As one man we rushed through the locker rooms and endless corridors filled with sweaty handball players.

When we got out on the steps, the place in front of us was already black with people and above them waved a sea of red banners.

The first one said:

HANDS OFF DAS RHEINGOLD

The next one said:

FOR ACADEMIC FREEDOM, WAGNER, AND SOCIALISM

I realized that this was a historic occasion.

7. A Number of Gods Descend
from the Machine. The Machine Remains.

Yes. I remember it as a happy time. And the days that now followed were the happiest of all. Here, where I sit enclosed by snow, in January of 1976, listening to the hoarse cries of crows in the cemetery where the naked branches can barely support the weight of the snow; here, where I sit in my cold study and can literally hear the thermometer creeping downward in the bay window; here, where I sit in a sleepy little town close to the North Pole; here, where I sit with a blanket across my knees, drinking lime-blossom tea and writing my querulous little poetry reviews, I remember those days as the very last days of my youth.

In 1861 Richard Wagner's friend, the great anarchist Mikhail Bakunin, escapes from his Siberian imprisonment. This was during the distant, happy time when it was still possible to escape from Siberian prison camps. He travels down the river Amur as it slowly frees itself from the ice, down shores edged with dwarf birch and stark osier.

At the end of June 1861, he boards the American freighter *Andrew Steer* in the port of Nikolaevsk. By way of Japan, San Francisco, and New York, he at last reaches London. Alexander Herzen sits in his apartment, listening to the quiet hissing of the samovar, and his wife knits in a corner of the room. Outside there's fall and fog. Monarchs reign; the Secret Police throw a huge net from the Urals to Portugal; the great radical movements formed in the middle of the century have been transformed into small sects that quarrel stubbornly and maliciously. Everything is very quiet. Everything is very melancholy.

And Mrs. Herzen knits, knits stubbornly with clenched jaws. Sometimes there's a wrong stitch, and she patiently unravels her knitting and goes on.

Then there is a heavy, characteristic knock on the door. Somehow they recognize it. They've heard it before. They open the door. It's true: there stands Mikhail Bakunin, large as life.

"At that moment," says Herzen, "we understood that the year 1848 never died in our hearts."

It was exactly the same way when we went out on the steps of Wood's Gymnasium and saw that the open space in front of us was a sea of people, red banners, and booming speakers.

At that moment we realized that the year 1968 had never died in our hearts.

Good lord! The university had had its share of the events of that year. The National Guard had laid siege to the campus for days on end, and the tear gas hung so heavily over the elms that it even penetrated into the classrooms. But that was all so long ago. People had adjusted. They had forgotten. There were new students and new faculty now. Tennis and football and racquet ball and courses in group psychology, defensive driving, and new life patterns, in organic farming and rural techniques, had completely engrossed their minds.

And now all at once everybody discovered that it's possible to say no, that getting angry is not necessarily a sign of psychic disturbance, that attack is permissible—in short, that it's all right to revolt.

One trombonist from the orchestra had taken his

trombone with him on the steps. Oh, how the brass shone in the fantastic afternoon light. And there was a tuba, no, not one but several tubas. And now they were playing, straight across the crowd of demonstrators: Tam-ti-ti-tam-ti-ti-daaa.

I wonder how many realized that it was the Siegfried Motif and that this was a way of saying that the old gods were dead and that all the old contracts had been canceled.

There were rumors that the National Guard had been called in, that the president was still locked in his office, that Governor Frisco would intervene personally and fire the whole Board of Trustees, but it amounted to nothing but rumors.

As the hours went by, the shouting crowds in front of the main building grew hoarser. Some students started to leave the campus simply because it was time to get something to eat.

I had temporarily shelved my plan for a serious talk with the great conductor Vico Varossi. The moment was not quite right.

New rumors reported that a gang with Texas flags had just appeared on the east side of the campus carrying large black banners with words like:

LONG LIVE VERDI: FUCK UGLY COMMUNISM
MORE ELEPHANTS ON CAMPUS: FUCK PER-
TURBER

It soon became clear that this was a gang from Mr. Frisco's Republican party organization, and they were beaten up and thrown off campus before they realized what had happened.

I walked aimlessly back and forth through the crowd,

made a brief visit to my own department, only to find it as empty as an Egyptian burial chamber. They'd all gone over to the English Department for deliberations. I went over to the English Department, only to find that the whole faculty was about to assemble in the big auditorium in Watts Hall.

On my way over there it struck me that it had turned quite dark in the last half-hour. A restless wind was rustling the elms. One of those tremendous Texas rainstorms was on its way, one of those downpours that make you feel the whole sky's a bathtub and you're sitting under the tub like a mouse, just where the plug is, and someone's just pulled the plug. There would be a flash flood; low-lying streets and roads would be inundated with running brown water.

The first lightning bolt hit with a thunderclap; the tree branches jerked violently.

Inside the big auditorium a bald professor with small gold-rimmed glasses was just analyzing the position of the university from a legal point of view, with special reference to the Constitution of the State of Texas. The guy sitting next to me explained that the liberals had just fucked up when they pointed out the connection between Verdi and the Italian Liberation Movement and that the whole situation was actually quite serious. One resolution after another had been read, but not a one had won universal approval.

Now the thunder boomed outside the closed curtains on the tall windows, the speaker lost himself more and more among Supreme Court case precedents, and wet umbrellas leaned sadly against the door, leaving rivulets of rainwater behind.

The afternoon was losing its cool.

I guess there's no sensible person who hasn't, at some time or other, thought about how different time can be. What I mean is that sometimes there are weeks or months, sometimes even years, when nothing special happens. You're in a certain groove, you've got your ordinary joys and sorrows and tax forms, Fourth of July and Christmas, and then you've got to do the taxes again.

Then when things start happening, well, then everything happens at once. Somewhere in my cubbyholes here on Blåsbogatan—if I remember correctly it's in a brown cardboard suitcase in the attic, with some old photographs and letters—I keep an old yellowed copy of *The Daily Texan*. Sometimes when I'm up there looking for the Christmas-tree stand or trying to fix the TV antenna, I happen on it, and I always end up sitting under the bare light bulb in the attic, giggling over the wrinkled yellow paper until someone calls up to me and says I've got to come down or I'll catch cold. Years later this paper still instills in me something akin to religious awe.

That's because it's the only valid argument I know for Strindberg's Powers, those strange punishing and encouraging gods *ex machina* who start warning and admonishing us as soon as we let them have even a little finger. One of my principal arguments against religion is that if we start believing in those kinds of powers, we can easily arouse them even if they've never existed before, because the human imagination has a strange faculty for conjuring up reality where, previously, there wasn't any. Who ever heard of Allah intervening in anyone's existence before Mohammed turned up? Who had the bad luck to be torpedoed before Jules Verne wrote *Twenty Thousand Leagues Under the Sea*?

82

This was the paper I pulled out of my mailbox around seven in the morning on December 13, 1974. It was the Feast of Santa Lucia, a day not much celebrated in Texas apparently. The rain had stopped around one that morning; deep in my sleep I'd heard it stop. Now a light, warm breeze was blowing, and it was already sixty degrees. I didn't feel quite right and leaned my head against the elevator door as I rode up again with my paper. There's an hour just after I wake up when I'm always slow to grasp things. Not even the blackest headlines become comprehensible until I've had my morning coffee. If I were as stupid all day long as I am at seven o'clock, I'd have spent my life in an institution.

I stared and stared at the newspaper. The whole top half of the first page was dominated by two large pictures. They were of Chairman Hugh Frisco and Dr. Geoffrey Gore, Chancellor and Vice Chancellor, respectively, of the university.

That was all right. It wasn't to be expected that yesterday's firing of the president would pass without comment. But it was quite impossible to understand the headlines. There was nothing about the president getting fired. Nothing about Wagner's *Das Rheingold*. Nothing about Verdi's *Aida*. Nothing about yesterday's violent student demonstrations. Nothing about elephants.

There was a smaller picture of a third gentleman on the same page. He had a sad, somewhat doggy look and huge ears. I had a strange feeling that I'd seen him somewhere before, but that was absurd. According to the caption he was Assistant Sheriff Gordon Hugh Smith.

I read the whole story and didn't understand a thing. What did they mean by an "immoral act"? What on earth was a "batter's box"? And what possible connection was there between Assistant Sheriff Gordon Hugh Smith and the Rhine Maidens?

And above all: why in God's name had the principal trustees of the university, Chairman Hugh Frisco and Dr. Geoffrey Gore, been arrested around three o'clock this morning on the order of the District Attorney of Travis County?

Even good news loses a great deal of its charm when it's incomprehensible.

I let my tired eyes travel down the page; they were caught by a picture of old ladies in San Antonio being carried away from a flooded parking lot by brave policemen in connection with yesterday's rain, and then another headline arrested my attention.

TWO HOURS BLACKOUT IN NATIONAL DEFENSE SYSTEM

In somewhat fuzzy and militarily understated language, it told of how the whole data system of the Strategic Air Command from Anchorage, Alaska, to the Canal Zone and from Bering Strait to Okinawa, had actually been out of order for two hours yesterday. Fortunately, the backup system at Alice Springs, Australia, had not been affected by the breakdown, which had probably occurred because the entire system, due to some as yet undiscovered programming error, had been overloaded with data. How on earth this was possible in a system with such enormous capacity the Pentagon experts weren't able to say as yet, but the Defense Department promised that the incident would not be repeated.

It was still quite early. I threw myself at the phone.

Professor Liz Hobstone's voice fluted merrily at the other end.

"Oh, isn't it *fun* that you're looking for Chris. He's spoken of you such a lot. He's always so *proud* when he's found a new friend."

"Hi there," said Chris.

"Hi," I said. "*I see from the paper that your Strindberg research is progressing.*"

"Oh well," Chris said, "it boiled up rather fast yesterday, I've never experimented with the whole national system before. It's got great capacity, and I got just what I needed. It's just that toward the end there was no room in the system for any of the other programs. There's nothing to get upset about, they're going to have a disarmament conference in Helsinki anyway."

"Watch out you don't get into any accidents," I said.

"I will," Chris said. "The rest is very simple. In a couple of weeks you'll have the third book about the Powers."

"OK," I said. "Good enough. Be seeing you."

I arrived at my department in good time and found the secretarial pool a boiling cauldron of laughing, talking, and generally excited professors, assistant professors, instructors, teaching assistants, and research assistants. It took me a while to find someone who was prepared to explain the whole thing to me.

This much was clear: the crisis was over; the president was saved and was the hero of the day; *Das Rheingold* was saved and the future prospects of the university were quite different from last night.

And all this thanks to Assistant Sheriff Gordon Hugh Smith.

This great guy—during the following spring, by the way, there were suggestions that he be made an Honorary

Doctor of Law, but I don't know whether it actually came to anything, because by then I was already far, far away—this great guy had been on his way home from the Third Police District around two in the morning, in a patrol car. It had been a hard night with traffic jams, reroutings, and car accidents in the wake of the flash flooding.

All of a sudden Assistant Sheriff Gordon Hugh Smith noticed two car lights, growing fainter and fainter, in the middle of the field of the university's baseball stadium.

In the belief that some kind of break-in was under way, he had driven up to the main entrance, whose aluminum gates had evidently been forced open by a car which had been driven straight at them. He had driven right onto the field and had jumped out of the car with his gun drawn and then discovered a huge Cadillac with dark windows and a buckled front bumper parked right in the middle of the infield. In the car was a gentleman asleep at the wheel, drunk as a skunk. This gentleman, once he'd been roused—which proved no easy task—and asked for his driver's license, turned out to none other than the Vice Chancellor of the university, Dr. Geoffrey Gore.

Fifteen yards further into the darkness Assistant Sheriff Gordon Hugh Smith found another couple of people, namely Texas Senator, Doctor of Law (Hon. Caus.) Hugh Frisco engaged in committing an immoral act with a waitress from a nearby hotel, inside the batter's box.

"What on earth is 'the batter's box,'" I asked.

In baseball, explained the research assistant, there is a pitcher, a batter, and a catcher, among other individuals.

86

The pitcher and the catcher are on the same team. The pitcher throws his ball as hard and straight as he can toward the corner of the diamond where the catcher is standing. But between the catcher and the pitcher there's the batter, a member of the other team. He's the one who's supposed to hit the ball with his bat and hit it in a wide arc, far enough so that his teammates can run to the next corner, which is the next base.

The batter's box is the place where, according to the rules, the batter has to stand. It's a sacred place, surrounded by powerful magic. At the baseball field in Austin players like Babe Ruth and Lou Gehrig once swung their bats.

"The scandalous thing, the thing that means we can count on having gotten those two Mafia bosses off the Board forever," said the departmental Goethe expert, "isn't drunken driving and breaking and entering and immoral behavior and messing around with women in general. The whole city is used to the two of them taking that kind of liberty, and they've got lawyers to get them out of that kind of difficulty. There are always voters who like their local politicians to do that kind of thing. That shows they're tough guys. No, what makes this into something serious, actually a catastrophe, for them, and what'll make them moral lepers as far as this city is concerned, definitively and for all time, that's something else, and that's their arrogance."

"What do you mean, arrogance," I said, feeling as stupid as a baby.

"But don't you know," said Pat, our best-looking secretary, with a slight blush.

"What?"

"Don't you know that the best batter on the home team always sleeps with a girl on that spot the night before a big game. It's ancient tradition. That's what makes this into a *horrendous* scandal. Can't you understand that?"

"You Texans," I said, "are more interesting people than a European thinks to start with. Australian aborigines and desert Arabs look different. You look like us, dress like us, but actually you're a strange, fascinating people."

"Listen to that. *You're making progress*," the Goethe expert said.

Of course you wonder what happened to the tennis players. O.K., I'll tell the story as well as I can.

I met Abel a few more times at the tennis court. He was a fascinating teacher, and slowly but surely I started to understand that what he was actually teaching me wasn't tennis at all but the art of living, with tennis as his medium.

Later that spring he entered the WCT and beat Rod Laver in the finals 6–2, 6–0, 6–3. I've often wondered how he used his prize money. I can't imagine anyone in the whole world who ought to get along better without money than he. He was related to the great teachers, Gunnar Ekelöf, the Japanese Zen monks, the ancient archers, and the Australian aborigine medicine men.

I keep his sayings in a small notebook, all about the emptiness of the serve, the eternal now of the soaring ball, that in reality you are no one, about the thought of the ball that's gone never being allowed to poison the thought of the one you're just about to hit.

Some time, toward the end of my life, I'm going to publish his sayings with an extensive commentary. But only when I've reached such a state of maturity that I am able to penetrate the secret, innermost significance of those sayings which, superficially, deal with topspin, slice, and overhand-backhand volleys.

Some people might wonder—you might as well admit it, hypocritical reader—about the small, fantastically skillful girl in bleached jeans called Polly.

Well, I saw her briefly once again, just once.

It was an evening a few months later. It was the evening of the first performance of Wagner's *Das Rheingold*, a performance moved to the City Concert Hall because of the enormous turnout.

The first act was over. Doobie (she had somehow made up with the conductor; perhaps he stopped eating garlic, or else his musical sense came to the fore—what would I know?) had been simply brilliant as Flosshilde, soaring across the dark green stage from an invisible plastic line, up and down and back and forth, like some kind of aquarium fish, with the other two Rhine Maidens, Woglinde and Wellgunde. The applause at the end of the first act never seemed to want to stop.

In the lobby all that Texas owned of learning and wealth and splendor was gathered by the champagne buffet, the gentlemen splendid in white dinner jackets and the ladies, the blue-haired ladies, loaded with jewels and rhinestones, fantastic young beauties with raven hair hanging loose and the kind of exquisite milk-white skin that no suntan can spoil.

I elbowed in here and there, listened to what people thought about the first act, put in a good word for

89

Flosshilde with the reporters from the local papers, and lightly criticized the tempo of the Italian conductor toward the end of the first scene.

Suddenly, squeezed between two convivial champagne-drinking groups, I felt a very strong, very slim hand coming from somewhere behind me, gripping me tightly by the wrist, and pulling my wrist toward itself. I immediately recognized that warmth and turned around quick as lightning.

There, in dazzling white organdy, weighted down with diamonds, with a tiara that would have made a member of a European royal house faint with envy, was Polly. Quite simply, she looked like a princess. I made a deep bow and kissed her hand. Somehow I felt that she had conferred a favor on me by showing herself to me for a moment in her true shape. That was all.

And now I suppose someone will ask how that damn Strindberg project turned out. Not well. Or perhaps one might say it turned out all right.

For one thing, Bill, my graduate student, the one who had started the whole thing, came in one day and told me he'd decided to drop everything.

"Good heavens," I said. "But what are you going to do?"

"I've been accepted to the Harvard School of Business Administration."

"Good for you," I said. "Have a nice life. Remember to keep your feet warm and wear a woolen muffler. Harvard isn't like here. Harvard's cold."

Another reason was that Chris got fired from the Strategic Command Center. It had nothing to do with the overload, not at all; he's a good worker and knows what he's doing. It was simply that he participated in the big Wagner demonstration and happened to be in a picture that was all over the papers. He's with two friends, and they're carrying a big banner that says:

GIVE US THE TWILIGHT OF THE GODS AS WELL!

That made the government dig into their archives, and that in turn led to their finding out about his past in SDS in the late '60s.

He got fired with thirty minutes' notice, and, as he himself says:

"I didn't have a chance to remove the program, and if nobody else has removed it it'll keep on going until hell freezes over."

Anyway, things turned out much better than expected for Chris. He got a job almost at once with a Las Vegas consortium that needed a young expert willing to specialize in the IRS data machines and their possible malfunction. I think the research program was called something like Planned Insecurity. (By the way, I've noticed that that particular conglomerate has opened a branch office at the corner of Asögatan and Ringvägen in Stockholm; well, there are a lot of multinational firms nowadays.)

Neither thing was decisive. The really fatal thing is that I've never found Pietziewzskoczky's *Mémoires d'un chimiste* again. I've written to every library of any size all over Europe, I've looked through pounds of catalogs from antiquarian bookstores, all to no avail. The volume that Bill dug up that fall from a pile of discarded chemistry books must be an extremely rare copy. That's a shame. But I do have the book's Gödel number. It's a twelve-figure prime number, raised to another, sixteen-figure number. Theoretically it looks like any old telephone number, and it tells me nothing.

In brief: it was a happy time. It ended. I packed my bag, mailed my bike home, gave my rackets to the neighborhood children, and boarded a plane. A gray, damp, very warm cloud cover hid the whole city, the whole county, on the morning I left. A few friends waved good-bye to me at the plane: Doobie, John, Joe, Chris, and Larry.

Four hours later I stepped out of another plane in Santa Barbara, California. A mild scent of burnt lavender, of the Pacific, of the orange blossoms of California was in the air. I inhaled its mildness. It was over. Soft waves thundered in the distance. Then other adventures began. But that's a different story.

But the thought of that lone computer, buried one hundred and fifty feet underground in the Texas desert, equipped with the experience of a corporal and the mathematical genius of an Einstein and a Kepler combined, desolately ruminating year in and year out on August Strindberg's Powers and running through, over and over again, the drama that once was acted out at the Hotel Orfila in Paris, in the 1890s, the whole drama with all its variants, with all the alternative dramas and possible complications—sometimes that thought gives me a twinge of bad conscience.